STONES

The Swiss Library

STONES or *The Destruction of the Child Karl and Other Characters* Erica Pedretti
THE BOTTOM OF THE BARREL Plinio Martini
REVERIES OF A SOLITARY WALKER Jean -Jacques Rousseau
GREEN HENRY Gottfried Keller (in preparation)
TWENTIETH-CENTURY SWISS SHORT STORIES edited by H.M. Waidson (in preparation)

The Swiss Library is a new series designed to make available in English translation classics and contemporary writing from the literatures of a small, highly cultured European nation which has done much to fructify the world. Many Swiss writers are thought of as belonging to the traditions of Germany, France and Italy because Switzerland shares three of her languages with these countries. The publishers gratefully acknowledge the advice and assistance of the Cultural Department of the Swiss Embassy and of the Pro Helvetia Foundation in producing this series.

The Swiss Library

Erica Pedretti

STONES

or
The Destruction of the Child Karl and Other Characters

translated by Judith L. Black

JOHN CALDER · LONDON
RIVERRUN PRESS · NEW YORK

First published in Great Britain, 1982, by
John Calder (Publishers) Ltd.,
19 Brewer Street, London W1R 4AS

and

First published in the USA by
Riverrun Press Inc.,
175 Fifth Avenue,
New York, NY 10010

Originally published in Germany, 1977, by
Suhrkamp Verlag, Frankfurt am Main

British Library Cataloguing in Publication Data

Pedretti, Erica
Stones.—(The Swiss library)
I Title   II Veränderung. *English*
III Series
833'.914[F]   PT 2676.E3
ISBN 0 7145 3929 5

SUBSIDISED BY THE
Arts Council
OF GREAT BRITAIN

SUBSIDISED BY
Pro Helvetia
ZÜRICH

Typeset in 11pt Plantin by Margaret Spooner Typesetting, Dorchester,
Dorset.
Printed and bound by

Printed and bound in Great Britain by
Robert Hartnoll Ltd Bodmin Cornwall

STONES

I sat there, and the train
drove, destroying my frontiers, deep
through my body,
suddenly it was the train of my childhood,
the early morning mist,
the bright and bitter summer.

Pablo Neruda

When I shut my eyes and try to forget that I know where I am, try to forget that I'm not just a passer-by, not just on holiday but that I've come to live here, that I might even get to feel at home here one day, soon:

when I shut my eyes before the façades of this old-town street and take in only the sounds and smells like I did that first time when it was all strange to me, when I had no idea I might be staying here for years so there was no need to think about whether I could ever like it here or not:

all the loud conversations from window to window and down on the street; the calls in Spanish, Italian, mostly Spanish or Italian-sounding French, the music from many loudspeakers turned up full, the bel canto, life, the noise of cars and motor bikes, tooting, squealing brakes, and with all this the stench of exhaust fumes mingled with the smells from many kitchens, mostly onions and garlic:

I could believe I was in a Mediterranean town, somewhere in Apulia, Molfetta perhaps or Lecce, anywhere in the south, anywhere but the canton of Bern. And just like in Molfetta, or was it Trani, I am overwhelmed by the desire to immerse myself in this way of living, a way of living so foreign to me, to learn all I can about the people here, to explore their way of living for myself, as much as I possibly can.

But when I open my eyes and look around the room in which I'm sitting, the papered walls with their pattern of leaves and flowers still showing even after two coats of paint, clearly here, faintly over there, the pale green painted cupboard in front of me, the pale green window and door frames, the shiny paint of the ceiling panelling which fades from green to light ochre after the first beam and which is cracked and black from all the dust which has accumulated on the corners and the edges and in the gaps between the boards and which has blistered above the stove pipes or which is already flaking off, when I look at the worn flowered curtains and all the other things in the room left by Madame Serova, the old Russian lady who lived in this room before me, when I look at all the things in this room which aren't to my taste, like the deep red and black enamelled bowl with its plastic flowers embedded in pebbles, but which remain unchanged after two years of living here, because as time goes by my resolve to tear down those curtains, to throw away the black and red bowl, to get rid of everything I don't like, has gradually left me:

when I open my eyes I realize that I have become immersed here, that there's no point any more, as there was two years ago, in wondering whether and to what extent this could ever become a lifestyle for me. Just a few sentences, a page of words and my situation has been transformed. That desire to immerse myself in life here is now constantly threatening to turn against me, has been transformed into the fear of drowning.

I wouldn't be the first person this has happened to. That's why I'm leaving the cupboard closed for the moment. Along with the linen, a spare set of curtains, these with garlands on, and various files of old, unanswered correspondence, off-prints, my book proofs and other work and their reviews, there's a whole drawer of papers belonging to the dead Russian lady. Nothing important, nothing in particular, Madame Serova's relatives took all that before I arrived. Just a stack of Russian newspapers printed in New York, a few packets, still unopened, of a Russian weekly from Melbourne, UNIFICATION, a photograph album with several photos ripped out and various colour pictures of Swiss holiday resorts, printed on cardboard, some of them with shaky, uneven Russian handwriting on the back, prints of rural scenes, of a *dacha*, a low, thatched farmhouse on a calendar for 1972. The calendar is intact, none of the pages have been torn off.

Just as I couldn't take her patterned curtains down, I haven't been able to throw away her things which were around the flat, things the old emigrée seems to have treasured; I haven't been able to clear the place she belonged to of the things which belonged to her, haven't been able to rid myself of these reminders or of the old lady herself. Everything has been stowed away in this cupboard for two years now, the key turned twice in the shield-shaped lock with its badly varnished brass plate, removed, mislaid.

I've been mislaying all sorts of things recently and I waste a great deal of time searching for them. As I search I remember my grandmother; I seem to be getting like her, she who was always searching for keys and the names of her grandchildren and children: Grete! Helga! Heiner! Kurt! Erica! Find my glasses for me, please! I'm wasting more and more time searching for words and sentences and now I'm searching for an excuse to get away from the paper on my desk in front of me, from the typewriter, from the untidy pile of letters and notes and manuscripts, searching for a way out of this room, searching for words to describe the next room, groping my way through the dark kitchen, lit only by light from the inside windows, into the even darker corridor. The bluish light of the neon tube flickers on and off, as always, as if trying to make up its mind whether to come on or not, I'm half-way down the stairs, on the first floor, before it lights up.

I step out into the street and, as so often, when I reach the station, which is only a short distance away, I get into the first train that stops, I don't mind which way it's going, the scenery is beautiful in both directions, I love the view out over the lake and the old town with the castle on the far shore, the colour of the reeds in front of the strip of land which leads out to the island, the terraced vineyards in the background look reassuring. Often I don't notice the scenery, nor the people in the carriage with me; just words in front of me, titles, an article in a newspaper on my seat, or the page of a book, a verse.

I usually get out at the first or second stop and walk down to the lake, so I can walk home later along the lakeside, or rather past the grounds of the properties along the lakeside, or I climb from the station up to the woods, or I walk back through the vineyards half-way up the hillside. This time I go straight from the second station to the little harbour, where I sit down on a bench under the plane trees, look out over the lake and listen to Frau Gerster, the old lady who seems to have made this bench her regular haunt.

'That's where the growths come from, I think, from the stones. It happens quite suddenly, they can appear in less than thirty hours. He swallowed a stone once and he wouldn't eat for a few days after that and I said, there's something not right there, he must be ill. His father had the same thing and died when he was seven. The vet said he couldn't understand it but he didn't say anything to me about the father. It wasn't until later, unfortunately, not until afterwards that I phoned the man who bred him. Then I went along to the vet, he's one of the best. At first he said: It's his appendix, he's got a ruptured appendix, and he said he'd operate. And he x-rayed him and said: No, he's got something in his stomach, a stone. Then he gave me something for him to take, very fine, slimy, you know, just like pitch, for his intestines. Then, for two or three days, he tried really hard, he strained and strained and strained and strained, and every time we went out he tried straining and straining. We felt really sorry for him and I carried him around because he was in such pain, and then, suddenly, in the kitchen, he pushed one more time, there was a thud against the kitchen cupboards and there was the stone. That's where the growths come from, you see, because as he pushed the stone was forced along the intestines, right through everything, and it strained them. So when I see the boy, Karl that is, throwing stones, I always tell him: You musn't do that, you'll make the dog ill. Of course, you could say it's hereditary, the father had it as well, but who knows. And they do prefer stones to balls. The father liked stones as well, who can say that's not where it came from. They came quite suddenly with me as well, they formed in less than thirty hours, five of them I had, stones that is, they managed to loosen four of them and one had to be removed. It was all because of Karl, that's the boy we had ever since he was eleven years old who used to help me with my boats, hiring them out, cleaning them, doing the shopping, all that kind of thing; when he was a schoolboy my place, the boats, were a kind of refuge for him. And he was always nice to me, he could always get anything out of me. That's what made it such a terrible disappointment for me.

That's what they told me at the hospital. It came from all the trouble and worrying, over little Gero and Karl's thieving, and then later there was the accident on the railway. Everything mounted up, it all came at once and made the stones form, and those are the really dangerous ones. More dangerous than the kind of stones you have inside you for a long time because those are round while the others have got jagged edges. He also got jaundice because his bile ducts and the exit from his stomach were blocked by the growths. So the bile went into the liver and then into the stomach, so it was going in the wrong direction. For two months. His eyes were all yellow. I used to take him out every evening and his stools got worse and worse, yellower and yellower. He lost all his energy and he wasn't eating anything, so we started giving him tinned food, the kind you give to babies, all soft, but it wasn't enough, it didn't give him enough nourishment. This went on until the vet said: It's a ruptured appendix. And the worse I got the more ill he became, he must have sensed it, if his mistress wasn't there any more he'd get bored, he'd have

pined away even if he hadn't been ill. They say dogs have a
fifth sense, or is it a sixth, and there's nothing you can do
about it, they're born with it. It's the extra cells they've got, in
their brains. On the other hand, they haven't got some of the
cells we've got.'

'On the other hand dogs haven't got some of the cells we have
got, they probably see things differently.'

Unfortunately, says Mademoiselle Alice who has lived on
the first floor for twenty-six years, unfortunately she had to
give up her dog, a lovely spaniel, years ago because of the
neighbours who couldn't stand it barking. So there was no
smell of dog left in the building, no traces, Frau Gerster's dog
undoubtedly smelled and saw our staircase differently, more
enthusiastically than we did. He had clambered up those
steep, wooden steps many a time, for Frau Gerster had
cleared out the flat of the old emigrée, Madame Serova's flat
after she died, for the refugee organization. The walls of the
stairway and the corridor are painted khaki, a speckly green,
to shoulder-height, what was once white above this is now a
patchy grey, full of cracks and holes.

I'm not going to sleep in this grotty place, said Carolina,
my youngest, on our first evening here.

You're brave, said Mademoiselle Alice, nothing in the
building had been repaired for thirty, maybe forty years, she
told us, she had installed the boiler herself, like the oilstove,
and painted her own flat, she paid to have a stove put in so at
least she had some way of heating the place. The loft was
rotten, the Spaniards used to hang out their washing up there,
she had never dared go into the loft.

But it's the loft which interests us most about the building,
because it could be converted into a good studio with a bit of
alteration. My husband is a painter and sculptor, we could
probably have found other, nicer flats in the area, but none
with a studio.

We, that is my husband Gian, myself, three children still at school and two who come home in the holidays, moved temporarily into the flat of the old emigrée who died two weeks before we arrived. *La vieille dame soviétique*, the plumber calls her.

There were pink carnations on the kitchen table, Frau Gerster had put them there to welcome us. We also get a lot of practical tips, and from the hour-long conversation between Mademoiselle Alice and Frau Gerster here at this table we learn all about the electricity prices, peak and low-rate charges, the best places to shop and all kinds of less useful information, the moment we arrive. Tomorrow Frau Gerster is going to bring us some cake, she informs us, and neither is the considerable walk going to deter her from popping round to see us over the next few days, because the dog has to be taken out anyway, it makes you tough, you have to go out in all the wind and rain, there's no avoiding it, you just have to if you want to be humane to the dog. And even though, as she's always the first to admit, she's a sturdy build, fat in other words, the two flights of steep stairs didn't deter her in the least from paying us regular visits, with her dog on its lead, to see how we're getting on. The dog was called Gero.

'Gero. That's Hans in German. There was a Japanese film with a boy called Gero in it, and as we didn't want to call him Hans we called him Gero. How should I put it — animals are all so different, their characters are all so different and you're the one who can shape that character if you've had it since it was little, you can tell at once: the way they behave depends on how you treat them. Like dog, like master. You often hear people saying: Our dog is so intelligent. You can be sure they are the ones who spend a lot of time on the animal, who talk to it. That's not going to be the kind of dog who's made to sit out in the yard all day, who's only there to guard the house and never gets any attention, apart from some food occasionally, those dogs aren't going to be as alert. It's the same with people. The kind you can talk to are the ones who'll get somewhere while the others stay right where they are, at the bottom. So if a boss knows what he's doing he won't get rid of the talkative ones, the intelligent kind, those are the ones they'll hang onto; basically they like that sort, if they're not cocky, that is, because the boss knows: I've got someone here who'll help me get my ideas and my policies across to the others, so we can all work together well. It's a question of doing the right thing and they won't throw someone out who's good at talking, he's the one they'll keep. And if you've got a better job available you'll probably even promote him, because of his intelligence, if you've got someone from the work's committee who's good at talking, if he's the kind of person you can discuss things with, he's going to go far, he could even get into the Government.

You have to work at him, you have to talk to him, just like with a child. And you have to give them fish, dogs that is, it feeds the brain. Children too. They've got a lot of human characteristics, if you really study your animal you can see all kinds of similarities, they've got a lot of the character and intelligence humans have got, that's why it's interesting to watch them.'

I was to find out a lot more from Frau Gerster, learn a great deal from her, but right then I was very tired. The move, the journey here from the Engadine, getting used to the change of air, the different light, the change from rural peace, or what we remembered later as being peaceful, to all the noise of the town, the new smells, none of this was very easy.

I had also envisaged, indeed wanted, an empty flat, so we could settle in here with only the bare essentials and have lots of empty space, half-empty rooms. But, most considerately, Frau Gerster had left us everything she thought we might find useful, she obviously thought she was doing us a good turn with Madame Serova's carefully preserved furniture and cooking pots and clothes.

I was greeted by something I had never set any store by, something we'd never even had in my parent's house, something the looting Russian soldiers at the end of the war had asked for in vain, searched room after roomm for: *zjelaja garnitura*. And here it was, the complete 'suite of furniture', the fitted bedroom with matching beds, bedside tables, chamber pots, dressing tables and the portraits of a youthful Monsieur and Madame Serov. She was a beautiful woman once, my husband has hung her picture in his studio.

Frau Gerster got the bedroom all ready for us, made up the beds. But we were loathe even to cross the threshold and we installed ourselves in the other room, the one I'm sitting in now, behind the kitchen on the other side of the narrow house.

We are unable to sleep that first night. At two o'clock in the morning we get up, take Madame Serova's pictures and a big ugly mirror down from the wall, carry the cupboard with the glass doors and the two plastic plants out onto the narrow corridor and lay the mattress on the floor, between the bare, flowered walls, which are now decorated with dark patches instead of holiday views. A young Spanish couple who used to live up on the top floor, the third floor, and who now have an almost identical flat next-door to us come along next morning to see if there's anything there they can use.

In the old days you used to know everything about everyone else, Frau Gerster tells us on her first visit. She studied my husband carefully, sized up his build and then fetched Monsieur Serov's overcoat, which fits him like a glove: You'll just have to alter the buttons, it's a very good coat. I manage politely to decline Madame's Serova's good coat.

Next to me on the window-sill there's a long, narrow cushion covered in orange-coloured plush. Everyone in the street has cushions like this one of Madame Serova's, soft cushions on the window-sills which you can lean on, there are people leaning out of most of the windows, usually old ladies during the day and in the evening men too, whole families, often looking out at the street for hours on end, chatting with the neighbours or passers-by.

It used to be one big happy family here in the town, says Frau Gerster: 'Just like it was with us in Seewyler in the old days, and there was nothing wrong with that, oh no, people didn't spy on each other, it wasn't like that. Now and again you'd say: How are you, and you'd ask if they had any problems, if anything was wrong, or you'd notice that their clothes were looking a bit worn, that kind of thing, and you'd think to yourself: Rather than throw my clothes out I can give them to them, to that family. But you sorted through them first, you didn't just hand them over as they were, you made sure you didn't give them anything tatty, you only gave them things that were in good condition. You could always tell if people were careful with their money or not, if they took care of their things, you can tell that at once, you don't have to go into people's houses to see that, you can tell from the kind of people they mix with, the way they behave. Take the young Spanish girl who used to live above Madame Serova, she was good at sewing so she took the Russian lady's clothes and some other bits and pieces. I had to clear the flat out and clean it all after the funeral, young Karl helped me. We put the beds and everything else from the front room on the pavement in front of the building and it hadn't been there half an hour before lots of it had gone, all kinds of things, it all disappeared, clothes, everything, you couldn't help laughing! I suppose it was the best way, the things were taken by the people who needed them most. And the gold rouble, when the people from the council asked me about it I said: I don't know anything about it, and young Karl didn't take it either or he'd have told me, he'd have let something slip because in a way he was still terribly childish. He did rummage through her things, poke about a bit, he found a little earring but he didn't take it.

I hardly knew her before, the old Russian lady that is, until I had to come over here for the doctor one day. When her husband was alive they used to come over to see the Jarjems who lived below us, as far as I could tell they were a happy couple, got on well with each other. He could speak German and he used to get everything, he did all the shopping. But he did have some funny ideas, I think that's because his arteries were hardening, he used to imagine that he'd been an officer. The Jarjems came from the same village, so he knew him, he did his military service with him and he knew he hadn't been an officer, that he'd had an even lower rank than himself. But if you'd seen him, the way he carried himself, just like an ex-officer, very high and mighty. He died two years before her and she died of grief, yes, she pined away, or it might have been from boredom. The Jarjems told me, they used to come over to her place quite a lot because she had a television set. Later on Madame Jarjem used to do her shopping for her, with this self-service it doesn't matter whether you speak French or German, or just Russian, with self-service you just take what you need, self-service shops are really good for foreigners who have no language. Anyway, Madame Serova had no one left, just two lady friends and that's why she lay on the floor for days, she must have knocked but the Spaniards upstairs didn't hear anything and the one below didn't notice anything because of the radio, she's always got it on. They never had much contact anyway, the woman downstairs is terribly stand-offish, she only ever said 'good morning' to her once in a while. But the Russian lady probably couldn't say anything much, nothing at all probably for the first few days, I think she just lay there paralysed on the living room floor. A stroke. All alone for days on end, she could easily have starved to death. If you haven't got any one, not a soul, not even a dog. When I think of what Gero used to do, how he used to watch over my mother! That was because of, how should I put it, because of the trust we had in the dog, he thought: I've got the responsibility, I'm the one who's responsible for my grandmother. Sometimes she'd give him a piece of chocolate, he really loved that, or some sugar, to thank him. Maybe, that's what made all the difference, why he dashed off the moment she said: Go on! Fetch Mummy! And he'd be off in a flash, there was no stopping him. He could open the door with his nose, he could even open the front door himself.

Anyway, it was a stroke. And our Russian lady started to wonder why she hadn't been round for so long and she caught the train over to find out why and found her lying there like that, and Madame Jarjem and the other friend got Madame Serova onto the couch and called the doctor. And he saw me and told me what had happened and he said to me: Frau Gerster, could you possibly come and give me a hand? The women were just sitting with her, they hadn't done anything else for her, nothing at all. He felt she couldn't be allowed to stay there in those things, in all that mess, she wasn't capable of doing anything for herself.

But she was quite clean otherwise. This was Monday afternoon and he got the ambulance to come on Tuesday morning, I got her all ready, washed her, put clean clothes on her, and she kept her clothes, she didn't want her clothes to be taken away. She could only speak Russian, the other one too, which made things difficult for me, even down at the hospital they couldn't talk to her. So I told the doctor: It's quite simple, just tell me what you want to ask her, he gave me a piece of paper, my tenant Monsieur Jarjem can speak a little German, he can translate it and we can send it back to you. Half past nine Thursday morning he rings me up, says she's not looking too good, and as I get to the hospital they've just taken her away, she'd died.'

I hardly knew her, had only met her once. I'd get to know her better in time, I'd learn Russian again, I had thought. We'd be able to communicate, she'd have someone around the place she could talk to. For I'd been told by the landlords that apart from Russian she could only speak Chinese.

The first time we came here to have a look at the town, the street, this old house, we rang Madame Serova's bell and there was no answer for quite a while. We had time to inspect the tall, narrow façade of the building with its plaster crumbling along one gutter. On the first floor a half-open shutter moved, or I thought I saw someone or something move behind it. From the windows of the neighbouring houses and the ones across the street there were several people watching us closely. We were just about to turn back when a light on the stairs flickered on; first we saw little slippers, black stockings, a black apron coming down the stairs, an old lady was carefully setting down one foot after the other, the second foot onto the same step as the first, and her round face was moving backwards and forwards as if she was shaking her head in disapproval as she opened the front door. With a defensive gesture and still shaking her head, she motioned us inside, as if trying to invite us in and ward us off at the same time. She was saying something, but it was an incomprehensible muttering which we followed, embarrassed and hesitantly, up the stairs.

With great effort, step by step she leads us on, her black patterned overall against the speckled green, unevenly painted wall, which reaches to her shoulders; on the step outside Mademoiselle Alice's door she pauses a moment, out of breath. Climbs on up to the second floor, her floor, feeling her way along the panelled wall of the corridor. We ask her, gesticulating, to show us the empty flat on the top floor. Madame Serova sighs and continues on her way, shaking her head, we climb up to the next floor and she mutters, as if passing comment on what she and we are doing here.

On this narrow stairway with the light getting dimmer and dimmer, it's more like descending down and down, floor by floor into a mine rather than climbing upwards, and from the mine's main shaft there are cell-like rooms branching off in two directions, I feel as if I'm entering another dimension, another time, one I've never been in before and which is as strange to me as the old, oriental-looking face by my side. As if we're encroaching upon her time, upon the domain of this foreign lady, the domain in which she enjoys her right of asylum, however cramped it might be and however disturbed by the neighbours whose language and affairs she cannot understand. Just as she does not understand now why we have rung her doorbell, something only her two lady friends ever do, and just as she does not know what we're doing here, what we want from her. I think I know how she felt even if I can't understand the full extent of her anxiety. What it's like when you haven't got a language. I know what it's like to live alone among foreigners who speak a foreign language and only know a few words of your own. My regret now, looking back, too late as usual, at not having done something. I could have brushed up on my Russian a little before our visit, could have looked through some of the key vocabulary. As a fifteen year old my survival depended for a while on a peculiar, rapidly acquired mixture of Czech and Russian, I muddled along, as they say. But something separates me now from what I once was, what I once knew and could do: the house, *dum*, yes, that's still there, I can see the sign *AOM*, the old signs on the doors, Krasnijdom, and *velky dum, stary dum*, but what's the use of 'the big', 'the old house', I can still say 'understand', 'not understand', *ne ponimaijem*, and 'good bye', I desperately search around for more words, for lost words which I know must still be there somewhere. What I knew then, however little, would be enough now, would enable me to reassure Madame Serova now.

The flat on the third floor is all locked up.

One floor down again. Madame Serova motions us with her arm into her kitchen, into the small, dimly-lit room with no outside windows, trapped between the corridor and the living room which we ourselves are later to use for almost a year, six of us most of the time, for cooking, eating, washing and working in. Madame Serova walks through the room and

I just have time to notice that the kitchen is crammed with too much furniture and crockery, I hardly dare take a proper look because of my embarrassment at intruding upon the helpless lady who cannot know it's not her flat we want; I only glance quickly at the room.

I can still see her standing there: she's smoothing her sleek grey hair out of her face, which is unlined, like the face of an old child, and she keeps twisting it away under the bun at the back of her head, and all the time she's shaking that head and looking at me, talking quietly to herself.

I shouldn't have said *dom* or *do swidanya*. Now my neighbour, her friend, who is also Russian, always jabbers away at me in Russian when she sees me, tells me I could learn Russian again with her, for her sake, and she says that Madame Serova hadn't accepted my *ne ponimaiyem*, hadn't believed I couldn't understand her.

When you've got no one, not a soul, not even a dog.

'She ought to have had a dog, Madame Serova should, one that could have pushed the door open with its nose, a good, intelligent dog, then something as awful as that would never have happened,' says Frau Gerster, but then there'd never be another dog like Gero.

'That's why I've never wanted another one. I'm still with him a lot, in my thoughts. And when I see a dog carrying and fetching a stick, it really hurts me inside. Then I always think, ours did that too. But I can't have one while I'm still not absolutely fit, and as time goes by you don't, how should I put it, you get used to being alone and you end up by thinking you won't bother getting another one. For the moment I don't want a dog at all. If I had one that wasn't as bright as Gero I'd be forever telling him: You are a stupid boy, old Gero was much cleverer than you, it just slips out automatically. Like you sometimes say to children: Your brother is cleverer than you, if only you'd try a bit harder, and I don't want that, not that.

We never trained him, because of the poodle in his blood, he understood everything very quickly. A piece of sugar on his nose and he'd throw his head back and catch it. It's the biggest mistake with children too, whether it's the parents' or the teachers' fault: when you tell them to do something they must do it, ten times I could say to him: go fetch this, go fetch that, and he'd do it, that's what they have to be taught, obedience, and if they can't obey it's going to have a pretty serious effect on their lives. He could do quite a few things, quite a lot without any training. He played football as well, he took the ball like this and struck it with his front paws so it spun away from him. He thought that it was fun. And it was fun for us to watch him. He had an amazingly keen instinct for everything, the kind you don't come across very often. If he liked you, you could do anything with him.

These days I just don't like walking as much, not for hours on end like I used to. Every evening when the children came home from school we used to take him out for a walk, when they felt like it, that is, they didn't always feel like going out.'

And what if they feel like going out almost every evening, my children, that is, but not with us. They sit with their friends down by the lake, smoking, playing the guitar; when the weather's bad and in winter they meet at the Café de la Gare or the Café de l'Union. At fifteen, sixteen and seventeen they travel to England, France and Greece, hitching some of the way, and I omit to tell Frau Gerster that my daughter spent a night in the station waiting room last week because she forgot her key and we didn't hear the door bell.

'But so many people make a mistake these days. You musn't think you can leave children to find their own way, that's all wrong. They must always know: someone's watching over me, I mustn't do this or that. Until they're seventeen, eighteen, until they leave school, that is. But that's a different generation already.'

One of the neighbours must surely have seen Susanna coming home.

And someone or other sees me coming home late, with Gian, as it should be, or on my own after a lecture or a meeting, sometimes with friends, laughing, in the early hours of the morning. Mademoiselle Alice stands at her open window, a bowl of water at the ready for the drunkards who venture too near her front door. She watches everything that happens at night.

Il faut se méfier, warns Mademoiselle Alice: don't go talking to everyone, *bonjour*, no more. Some of them seem friendly enough, but when your back's turned ... and if the police are always coming round making complaints it's because someone in the street is telling them things. And it's true, every few days we've got a policeman at our door because of the building materials, because of the sand we need for our alterations which is in a pile outside the building, or because of the crate of window glass, or he's asking what the children do when they're with their friends.

He hasn't been round for quite a while. Do people trust us more now?

Mademoiselle Alice doesn't approve of Frau Gerster's frequent visits. One should be careful. I should be careful.

'And how the world has changed since I was a child!' says Frau Gerster. 'For better or worse, that's hard, that's not easy to say. There's a lot more hunger for power around in the world now. One lot feels it has to keep the other lot under its thumb and that just makes for more unrest. If it wasn't for that there'd be a lot less dissatisfaction around, people would be a lot more satisfied with their own lives, and other people's. It's just like a stairway, at the top you've got the ones who've made it up there, in the middle you've got the ones who've made it as far as the middle, and at the bottom you've got the ones right at the bottom, there's nothing you can do about it, they might manage to climb a little way up but they can just as easily fall back down again, and that's where we are now, right at the very bottom.'

Last night, it was a lovely warm May night, I went down into the lower town, an ancient and very pretty town I'd been to before. I know its streets, I carry them around in my head like a map. I know every inch of the tram network, I know where the cables of the two *funiculaires* stretch out of the upper town, down over a high wall and terraced gardens with their lovingly kept flower beds and vegetable patches into the lower town, and I know at exactly which points, in which buildings the cabins come to rest. *Funiculaires?* A foreign word I don't usually use, which doesn't even look right here, I should have written 'cable cars'. I wanted to show my friends the castle and take a closer look at it myself, now I've heard so much about it, but it all seemed unfamiliar to me as we made our way there, even though (in the moonlight) the town below us was as bright as day. And I could remember a lovely bird's-eye view from the top. As we walked below through the twisting streets towards the Schlossgasse which leads up to the castle we kept coming up against the castle walls, and still we missed the main entrance and shook other, barred gates, even after a long detour during which we lost our way twice and got back to the front of the castle only with the greatest of difficulty via outhouses and hidden alleyways and courtyards. After searching around a long time in vain, when our feet were beginning to hurt, we retired to a room at the valley station.

It's a shabby, prison-cell of a room with the occasional homely touch, a blue sofa, a chair and a table, even if there aren't any curtains. 'And that's where we are now, right at the very bottom', I say and start, because I'm saying something that doesn't come from me. So I've settled myself in here for the moment and I show my friends quite proudly that I've got myself a room here too, like the other places I've lived in, even if it is a bit seedy. 'Of course,' says the lady I have to thank for finding me this accommodation, 'of course I went along to the office and I thumped on the desk, I really let them have it, I told them: That's what you're here for, for this kind of thing, the lady here needs a room and she needs it at once, so she can write! That's how I told them.' All it takes is confidence in your own ability to do it, says Frau Gerster; she, Frau Gerster, could also have got us into the Royal Palace and the Napoleon Room, she's disappointed we didn't see Leopold's toy railway under the arcades in the castle courtyard. Then she chases my friends off, says you can't let yourself be distracted like that all the time, you can't always have everything, you can't spend your whole time enjoying yourself, I should be writing now, and by that she means I should be writing *her* story, I ought to come to my senses, ought to see that life is work, she says: 'You've got two heads and that means two minds and the two minds must be able to work together.'

Then I wake up and realize with a shock that she has infiltrated my dreams, has implanted herself inside my head and won't leave me alone, not even at night. Realize that she wants to force me, even though there's really no reason for us to have anything to do with each other, to devote myself entirely to her, to her and her stories, to adapt them, write them. Two heads and that means two minds.

No, madame. I have something else in my mind, I'm trying to write, to continue something I started a long time ago in a different place. Not stories. I don't think I can achieve what I want to achieve with stories. I know too many people who put everything into stories, present everything in story form without realizing that stories have a life of their own, laws of their own, that they only allow certain points to be included while excluding other possibly more important ones, which will be dropped, forgotten. In the end what is life itself but a series of nice stories; funeral orations. What would life be otherwise? 'Life meant work for us,' I heard, 'and we still sang songs together, people still had fun, the wine harvest, that was fun for us, nature', I heard, and I didn't want to hear.

For I felt I could write now, I could see a scene, could see Eliette quite distinctly, and felt I had to draw her, describe her, right now, just a moment's more concentration — and with the feeling of being able to do it, the figure, the sentences ready in my head, I stood up and went to the window to see if the squealing of brakes meant there'd been an accident.

Across the way a black-haired lady is holding a pair of children's trousers out of the window, then a striped jumper, and is telling the neighbour to my right how much the clothes cost.

For his birthday! she calls across the street.

I didn't know you had such big grandchildren already!, the neighbour calls back to her.

My daughter will be twenty-six tomorrow! the black-haired lady replies.

I walk down the street, go to the station, and climb into the first train that comes along. An old man next to me is talking to the lady opposite, he seems to know her. He speaks in precise, regular sentences, like a schoolmaster with raised forefinger, and the woman he's talking to responds now and then with a 'yes' or just a nod of agreement. Unfortunately I can't close my ears as I can my eyes; my eyes don't have to witness his self-confident smile, I just bottle up inside me the terrible desire to answer him back. Two stops later when I get up, the old gentleman surges forward so he can get out first, but to my delight an even older gentleman with unruly white hair framing a patient, kindly face is standing a little way behind me.

From the station I go straight to the harbour, sit down on the bench under the plane trees again, look out over the lake and listen to Frau Gerster:

'Yes, you certainly get some stories to tell if you sit down here by the lake. There are so many people who come down here just to talk to me. The times people say to me: Tell me, what do you think?

Two heads and that means two minds, I think and look at her.

'Yes, trust is very important, even my face is important. And of course they know nothing will go any further. If people know that you can be sure they'll always confide in you, rich and poor alike.'

For a while I go on listening to what she is passing on and avoid answering when she asks me whether I really am writing down the things she's telling me specially so I'll write them down. Then I walk home through the vineyards. By tomorrow they'll be gone and forgotten, most of Frau Gerster's stories, but so will the other one, the one which had been so important and real to me a few hours earlier, something might have come of that if I hadn't gone to the window, if it had been allowed to surface properly, as it was so close to doing. Now it was already if not quite forgotten then so colourless that it wasn't worth starting all over again with.

'That's what you call unfinished business,' Frau Gerster would have said, and I'm going to be taking all my unfinished business to bed with me yet again tonight, I think, and the thought makes me cross. For I can no longer ignore the fact that her thoughts are now crossing my own, that I'm starting to think in her sentences, I'm even starting to use them.

It's an illusion, Eliette's still there, I contradict myself, she's walking a little unsteadily, as if hesitating before taking a step and wondering where to put her feet down, I am not too sure of her any more, but I can still see her. Everyone works in his own way, I don't have anything there 'ready' in my head, just a beginning and a general direction. 'What it takes is confidence and the determination that you can do it!'

I'm starting to hate Frau Gerster. For two years now I've been hearing that sentence, the one that taunts me.

For two whole years now I've been living in this house which is still as dilapidated as ever, in this old quarter where there are no trams and no cable cars and which was completely new to me. There's a castle up on the hill. For the first few months especially I observed things, I noted down what I could see from the house, what I can still see: part of this side of the street and the square on the other side, the north-east side of the street, the life I'm learning about even if I don't want to, the life I can't just observe but am part of, even if I didn't intend to be, while others in turn observe me. And the changes in this street, in this building and in me.

'And how the world has changed!' Frau Gerster maintains people used to be: 'how should I put it, more caring, people took more notice of their parents, I mean, people cared about them more, they realized it was their parents who fed them, you just had to get by as best you could so you helped out, you stayed with your parents, you were brought up quite differently from today.

Father was Italian, he came to Switzerland a long time ago. He trained as a locksmith and he'd worked on the Eiffel Tower in Paris, in fact, of all the workers they had there he was the last to die. We didn't know that but someone mentioned it in a speech at his funeral, and it was true. I didn't go into it any further though. In the '14–'18 War, before all the men who'd been at the front came home, that was in 1916, 1917, he got work at the Bern power station. He even helped with the installations, everything, then he went on to the big station at Hartneck. But later on when all the others came back it was a different story: We have to give the work to our own people, you can go now, and no one bothered that he'd got two children to feed.

But my mother came from Bern and she went back there. They told her: You can just go back where you came from! And she says to them: Look here, I was born in Bern! But they tell her that she's married now, that she'd signed a form and everything saying she was marrying a foreigner, so she's just got to face the consequences, there's nothing they can do for her.

We didn't get a penny, we had to fend for ourselves. My father used to go out fishing, he fished the river from Bern all the way to the Thielle and he sold the fish he caught, I went with him a few times, other times he'd go out picking mushrooms or berries, he knew a lot about mushrooms. In Bern he had to take them to the police to be checked but the police used to give him their mushrooms to check instead and that went on for quite a while because he was so knowledgeable about them. We lived in Stöckacker and all the people in Stöckacker used to come round asking: have you got this, have you got that, we went out gathering wood and gleaning and digging for potatoes and picking apples, we did everything. We never had to go to anyone for help. We used to deliver a paper, we used to walk miles with that newspaper.'

You're not allowed to shake your carpets out of the windows on the side of the building overlooking the square because the terraces on the first floor are like gardens, I am informed by Frau Gerster; yes, those terraces, it's just like having a garden in the summer, she tells me, in spite of the *bise* wind and even though, because of this wind, geraniums do better on the other side, on the street side. I also hear this from my neighbours the first time I hang the bedclothes out of the window. I should put my plants, is that a hibiscus?, on the other side. And Madame Serova's salmon pink geranium. On our neighbours' terrace there's a plush sofa which is covered over with plastic in the evenings and when it rains, and next to it there are several boxes of seedlings and gladioli in bud. Later, after the May frosts, Mademoiselle Alice tells me proudly that her new geraniums cost 125 francs.

Beneath the terraces there are the baker's store rooms, one

of the upholsterer's showrooms; he works out in the open below one of the other terraces, next to that there's the plumber. The children can watch the craftsmen at work or play at the fountain with plastic buckets and spades, between the parked cars, underneath a plane tree. And next to them people sit at tables in the 'conservatory' of the 'Au Progrès' restaurant: a small forecourt screened from the road by straggling ivy and two ferns set in tufa rock, in summer there are flowers between the ferns.

In the evenings and at weekends you see an astonishing number of motorcyclists, pairs or groups of them in their leathersuits, helmets in their hands or on their heads, visors up or, when they're seated on their machines and have started up their engines with a roar, visors down. Like gaily-coloured cavaliers of old they walk down the street with long, stiff strides, making either for the mechanic's diagonally opposite or for the 'Blue Bird', their bar on the corner, from where the music blares out across the street.

'Much too loud', says Frau Gerster. Yes, people were brought up quite differently in the old days, and also where love's concerned. 'Love for your parents and, well, all the other kinds of love too. Everything. We were never allowed to be all over each other, I mean, we couldn't just . . . we had work to do. Life meant work for us. We went out picking berries in the summer, and there was the wine harvest, that was fun for us, nature. And we all sang songs together, we had fun, but you didn't flirt about, no one wanted that kind of thing, you just didn't, everyone knew it was just something you didn't do. You can't always have everything. My brother-in-law, for example, young Paul, he was a good-looking lad and he fairly fell for our landlady, she was a real one for the men. And she had this illness, she had the same illness as him, where the white blood corpuscles get out of control, just like him, they get canny, the ones with that illness do. And they sent her to

the Zweisimmental for a cure too, and they left the san. and
went up to Oberstock and stayed up there a day or two, the
two of them, and of course they slept together, I don't really
know quite what went on. Afterwards the doctor said Paul
had got an infection of the testicles and that spread and he got
meningitis, and that was it. They said it could happen quite
suddenly, any time.

Once they've got that urge to stray in their heads it's bad to
hold them back. They're all the same.'

Ciao bella! the two young Italians call to my daughters from
the upstairs windows opposite. They've replaced the broken
panes with cardboard and as they've got no curtains you can
see, you can't help but see the whole room, a sofa on the left
and an iron bed on the right, the mattress without a cover, a
fridge, a camping table, bottles on the table and on the fridge.
In the evenings, after about six o'clock, they sit there with
their friends, singing or listening to the radio, or they lean,
singing, on the low iron railings in front of the windows, and
in the lamp light you can see that it's in fact two rooms, each
one scarcely six feet wide.

In just the same way you can see our mattresses on the floor
from across the way, the beer crates with most of our
belongings still packed away in them after six months here,
and if and when I make the beds. Mademoiselle Alice and the
postman can see our empty wine bottles on the stairs; when
we're eating we can only be seen from the flat above the bank
on the opposite side of the square if the lights are on and the
windows open. I know what sort of bedcover the Spanish lady
across the way has, I know its wavy patterns, just as the
Spanish lady has been able to see all our furniture ever since
we moved in and knows that the blue sofa is worn and
patched with badly matching material. She knows as much
about me as I do about her, she probably knows more. She
sees me going for the train to Biel every Monday morning and

coming back again at noon, just as I see her being picked up by an elegantly dressed woman in a car and being brought home a few hours later, Mademoiselle Alice knows the times and the days exactly.

Ask the Spanish woman, she advises, she'll help you with your cleaning as soon as your flat is ready, but not while it's looking like it does now.

I can hear when the Spanish lady isn't at work. And everyone in the street can hear me calling the names of my children, I hear the names of the other children.

You have to keep an eye on children, the girls especially but the boys too, Frau Gerster warns me: 'once they've started to stray that's it, they'll want to be off all the time then.'

Susanna and Martigna are allowed out until nine at latest.

Oh no, eleven, please! pleads Susanna.

Quarter past nine, says Gian.

We'll be back by ten at the latest! calls Susanna and is down the stairs and out of the door already.

Only two years ago they'd have come back punctually at quarter past nine, that was when it was still possible to reason with them, to talk to them about when they had to be back.

'I talked to him a lot. If you want an intelligent animal you have to talk to it a lot. I used to tell him stories when we were out, just as if he was another human being. The children gave him to me when my husband died, because my son was away and my daughter was too, she was in England and they said I wouldn't be as lonely then and it would also make me go out even though winter was on its way. You can't rely on children taking the dog out, they'll do it for the first month or so and that's it.

He didn't have a heart attack, my husband didn't, he had an intrax, that's the main vein from the heart which keeps pumping the blood back and forth, at the bottom of the heart; he blew his top at work, he got into a real rage, such a rage that the vein contracted and didn't open again, dead in seconds, they said, there's nothing you can do, you can't revive them, you can't help at all, it was a convulsion, he went all blue!

Yes, so when my husband died the children went off and I was left all on my own and I was pleased to have the dog. I used to go out with him every day, it really makes you hardy, it's good for you, it develops your resistance to coughs and colds, you have to go out in the wind and the rain, there's no two ways about it, it's something you have to do if you want to treat the animal properly, if you want to be humane. You have to think of an animal in just the same way as you would of a human being. A child who doesn't get any love, who's neglected, is going to be difficult, and a dog will be too. Every animal has a character there to be developed, it simply depends on how you bring them up, how you treat them.

Character. With some people it's in their nature, they just enjoy it when they can jeer at people and taunt them and bait them, it gives them a kind of satisfaction. And then there's the maddening kind who give you one story one minute and another one the next, until in the end you don't know who you are or where you're going, they're basically cheerful types, they just enjoy a good tease. Not in a nasty way, oh no. But you do get those, really nasty ones. We've got a woman like that here. But I don't know if she realizes what she's like. Does she do it on purpose, I've never been able to work that out, not in all the times I've talked to her. Some people are like that, there's something nasty behind everything they say and do, they jeer at you, make nasty comments, the moment they open their mouths something nasty comes out and the sort of person who's kind, who's considerate, will find it difficult to take, but they don't stop to consider whether you're the kind of person who can get over it or not. But experience teaches you whether you can take that kind of thing or not. With people you see a lot and you talk to often you can always tell what's wrong if they're in a bad mood. You can always ask them what the trouble is. But the other ones, the nasty ones, they're just born nasty and they're the same everywhere.

And many many people hit them. Never hit a dog, at least not with a stick and certainly never with his lead. It's better to take a newspaper and whack them with that. It doesn't hurt much but it does make them realize that they're being told off. So many people don't realize that, you can see it down by the lake. And if you've got children you should never have a dog as well, you can't be too careful, there are children who are as sweet as pie when grown-ups are around, but the moment the parents' backs are turned all their jealous instincts come out. They either pinch them or they pull their fur or pull them around, and then as soon as the grown-ups, the parents come back the children are as good as gold again, wouldn't dream of doing anything so horrid. I've seen a great deal of that, a great deal.'

Who can tell the extent to which the life people observe around them, especially for the older ones, eventually becomes life itself. A fat, elderly lady across the street lies at her window for most of the day. Like a marmot sitting there for hours on end, motionless, watching its burrow, invisible as long as it doesn't move or whistle or warn others when something hostile appears within its range of vision. She doesn't whistle, the fat lady doesn't, she gives me and most of the other passers-by friendly nods. What happens outside seems to mean more than her own life, which I find hard to understand. Does she recount her observations to someone, and if so, to whom? Does she see something that's new or strange as a threat or does she just accept change as it happens, which is quite imperceptibly usually, but then at other times, surprisingly suddenly, taking the people concerned unawares.

Thank goodness I'm not related to any of the old ladies or anyone else here, so that the conversations and observations don't mean direct involvement for me.

The Spanish girl next door is still the child of the lady across the street, even though she's married and is the mother of two children. She knows she's being well looked after but she's also under constant surveillance, her mother makes loud remarks about the dirty marks on her dress, darns the hole in her little granddaughter's sock, watches her daughter talking animatedly to a young man in the street, who is the young man? She knows how long she's out shopping, when her son-in-law comes home and when they put out the light at night. And as for the young husband, he's not just married to his wife but to her parents and her brother as well and he's in their charge. Anyone round here who can understand Spanish, and that's a lot of people, can understand the loud conversations between the mother and her daughter, all the family business.

Frau Gerster rescued a child from the lake once, her neighbour's little boy. 'He was three and a half then. And another time we rescued a boy who had slipped on the steps and his father didn't notice to start with. But when he did he shouted: Frau Gerster! My boy's out there! I can't swim! So I headed straight out there. In fact, he wasn't out of his depth yet. Just take your shoes off, you'll have enough air until your clothes are completely wet through and you'll be able to swim all right, of course, you're absolutely drenched afterwards. But the shock did something to the child and the older it got the more you noticed it until they had to send it to an abnormal school.'

Next door, on the first floor, there's a girl who's shut up all day while her parents are out at work. She's not quite normal. So she's one of the ones who look out of the window. You

never hear her talking and never see her laughing and people
say, Mademoiselle Alice says, that she spits at everyone she
doesn't like. You can give her window a wide berth if you're
not sure whether she likes you or not.

'Where we live people probably know even more about each
other than they do here or anywhere else, it's prettier too, and
when people have been there once they don't go away, or at
least they keep coming back, I came back.' says Frau Gerster.
'I lived in Nidau, I came back after ten years there, I'd got
married while I was away and came back with a family. But it
wasn't the same during the war, if you had a flat you had to
take people in. And I had my son in Nidau, we had a tiny little
flat, we were supposed to be moving but it was difficult to find
flats in Nidau, as it was everywhere. But as my mother had
this one empty she said to us: Don't move on somewhere else,
come home. He can get work in Biel. And my husband was
happy about it because the lake is so close here, in Nidau you
had to go to the canal. Right from the start, ever since we first
got married we've always had boats. The first one was just a
little flat-bottomed thing, the sort people used to have in the
old days and you had to row, just a little pleasure boat. Our
second one had a keel. We got an old engine for the flat-
bottomed one, it's in Lucerne now in the transport museum,
it's an Archimedes 2 H.P. We were able to sell it later on and
get a bigger one, a 5 H.P. We had the new boat a good many
years, until we came here in fact. He liked going out fishing on
Saturdays and Sundays. As the years went by there weren't
that many fish left, in '42, '43, until by '45 there wasn't
anything left to catch, and whenever he went down to the
lake, there weren't that many big boats there yet, about four
tourist boats a day, people were always coming up and asking
him if he would take them across to the island, and that's how
we hit on the idea of doing trips round the island. People
would come along at about one o'clock, the first boat went

across from here at quarter to three in the afternoon and came back about five, but they didn't want to hang around here so we did the trip round the island, we got back before three, everyone knew that. Here you are, you can read it in the paper, in what they wrote about me when I stopped:

' "THE QUEEN OF THE LAKE", that's me, that's what they used to call me, "is retiring. We are sure that many a tourist who missed the official lake trips still remembers her boats with gratitude. There were several occasions when Frau Gerster was not the only Queen of the Lake, however, because among the many VIPs she brought safely back to dry land and who entrusted themselves to her navigational skills were Queen Juliana of the Netherlands, the Prince of Liechtenstein, a Siamese princess and last but not least the Swiss federal fathers in corpore." '

Instead of being out on the lake in a boat I'm sitting here in my room. I haven't got any of the breathtaking views they extol in estate agents' windows, like the one from a house on a hillside; I look out over a street, house fronts of various colours, washing hanging from the eaves, roofs, chimneys, numerous television aerials, or a single tree, heavily lopped, in front of the newly renovated building which houses the cantonal bank and which is trying hard to look like a grand country residence, a chemist's shop with pointed gables, overrun by an ancient glycinia, and next to that the tall, grey building we call the Parisian house because it reminds us of Paris *banlieu*, of French suburban buildings. Far beyond this, in a gap, trees.

Oh, she'd much rather live in a house with a garden down by the lake, Carolina said the first time she saw this place. It wasn't difficult to explain to her why that isn't possible: we would have to give up our work, work we enjoyed, for a safer, more profitable way of earning a living, but first we had to be able to do so.

Instead of beautiful views here you see people. Just one of all the many different possible views, hardly giving you insight, just a superficial one perhaps. I mustn't start drawing too many conclusions from what I observe here!

And yet the way people behave, their gestures, their voices, the way they talk to each other when others can hear what they're saying, the way some people open their windows and let others see them in their rooms, let people watch them as they go about their everyday life, eating, watching television, all this proves that this is a lifestyle which clearly differs from those elsewhere, from life in one of the new satellite towns, for example, or in the house on the hillside.

Then they bought themselves a new boat, a bigger one, which her husband, Herr Gerster, used to navigate. 'And then we got a second one, because of the hotel. There were always groups coming to the Du Lac. Ten, eleven o'clock in the morning they'd arrive; one half of the party would go off bowling until midday, until lunchtime, and the other half was always offered a boat trip round the island. We could take nine in the boat, with me it made ten, if it was one of the big coaches we did the half hour trip. We could fit three more groups into the remaining half hours. My husband was at work, I had the boatbuilder to help me, I could go and get him if I wanted to, I'd get the two boats all ready and then I'd go and get him , and we paid him for the hours he worked. The two of us used to go out and my husband went to work in Biel, it wasn't worth him staying at home, there wasn't enough work for that. He worked in the factory, the last job he had was in the spares depot. He did his training with watches, anchor watches. But he wasn't able to go on with it because he sweated too much, that's why he went to the bicycle factory afterwards. It's tough work, he worked on the big press, the biggest one they had, he stamped out the mud-guards, it was tough work while the work with the watches was delicate, but he didn't mind as long as he had work. It wouldn't have been worth his while staying at home, Matthieu used to help me out as well, he was our old village policeman, I just used to see who was free to lend me a hand. My husband used to help on Saturdays and Sundays and in the evenings between six and eight, I used to tell the people who were waiting to hold on a while, that he'd be coming on the half six train, then I'd raise the flag on the boat so he'd know he had to come down to the lake. Here read this:

"After her husband's death Frau Gerster continued to expand her business. Anyone who wanted to be taken round the island, anyone wanting to hire a pedalo or berth or winter a boat, anyone who wanted to be set down anywhere along the lake went to the Queen of the Lake, who was also a member of the Lake Rescue Service." '

If only I wasn't such a stay-at-home, if only I got out of the house more and talked to people, not just Frau Gerster. I could write Madame Serova's friend's extraordinary life story, the story she told me once when we were drinking tea together. I haven't seen the old lady for ages, it suddenly occurs to me. I could write the plumber's story, the child hired out for board and lodging in the old way, who wants to take time off now to read Marx. I could investigate the life of the pale little boy I see staring out of a window every day, two floors below the window of the singing Italians. His nonna is making a dress in leopard-skin patterned material. She reminds me of my grandmother, yes, she looks like her, similar eyes, same hairstyle. She sews just as our grandmother used to sew and mend for us, but she sits there between the window and the curtain or she hangs washing up, mainly baby clothes, which my grandmother would not have done, and we greet each other in Italian when I too am hanging out my washing on our galetas. She calls: che tempaccio!

'It's almost friendlier here than in other places and we used to be like one big family in our village. If someone was in difficulties there was always someone around. There was one family with eleven children and you can't really say they were poor. If you saw they needed something you gave them clothes, shoes, if they had nothing to eat someone would bring them some soup and then someone always noticed these things and helped out, that's not how things are today.'

The difference between what I observe and what my neighbours observe, even Frau Gerster. I make many observations quite by chance, I see and hear many things I would rather not see and hear, rather not know about. And now, I'm observing so I can get to know things I've only heard other people talking about until now, so I can draw attention to them. That's what other people do, that's what Frau Gerster does too. 'So you can demonstrate something.' And help. 'No,' she says, 'it's not exactly prying on people, you just notice their behaviour, whether they're careful with their money or whether they spend too much, no, there's nothing wrong with it, of course not,' just lying there by the window and looking at what's happening, there's nothing wrong with that, I do it myself when I'm bored, when I'm tired, want to relax, I look out of the window like everyone else, aimlessly, curiously.

'Yes, someone always noticed if anyone was poor. So you couldn't say we had people who really were poor, Seewyler was famous for that. But then, when they started to build, there weren't any houses outside the villages then, each village, each town was a little place of its own still then, but because we had so many outsiders coming here everything changed.

The economic boom did it. It did a lot for our education system, for children and the way we lived, it gave us things we'd never had before but I say the most important thing is that you've got enough to eat and can pay your way, and if all people live for is having a good time, like people sometimes do, then they'd better pull their socks up if they don't want to lose their jobs, but they don't want to do that. A man with a family lost his job last autumn. When I asked him how he was getting on he said it was hard. So I told him: It's just a case of economizing a bit on the luxuries, but he said to me: I'd rather eat bread and cheese every day than give up my car. So I said: those who won't listen have to pay the price. We would never have got ourselves into that situation in the first place. If work was short you just cut back on a few things, and I think we were happier then, you could set up home for 1,000 francs in those days, not like today, 1,000 francs in those days would be about 10,000 today.

We both went out to work and his mother promised him some furniture, so she gave us a big Louis XV bed, a two and half person bed, and the old cupboard which I've still got and this table which I've always been careful with, then there were four of these chairs, no, we bought the divan afterwards, a few months later, and she gave us a chest of drawers and a kitchen table from her own flat, they were left over when they moved from Solothurn to Biel. And we made do with that, bought a few other bits and pieces over the years. The first thing we bought was a bicycle each so we didn't have to go by train, I've still got mine.'

Buying bicycles was the first thing we did too, second-hand ones from the mechanic across the way, later the children all got those yellow bikes you could use to cycle round the Biel Sculpture Exhibition on and which they sold off cheap when the exhibition was over. Sometimes we go off on the bikes, cycling for hours, that's how we got to know the area.

'Then he said: Now we've got our bicycles to get to work on, and for the sewing and mending, because I could sew and mend, he'd seen me doing my hand sewing in the evenings, he bought me a sewing machine, an "Adler", a new one, he paid

200 francs for it, that was a lot in those days. So we bought all this, and then he came home one Sunday morning and said: Look, I've found an old boat for 50 francs. He paid for it and brought it back, and as it was springing leaks every few inches between the boards, the caretaker helped him fix it and then we fitted the engine and from that time on we were always out fishing. We didn't go to the theatre once in all the eighteen years I was married, we never went to the cinema or the theatre, we always went off somewhere on our bicycles or went fishing, that's all we did.

I went to the theatre once, much later. It was a special performance for the King, for Fabiola and Baudouin, for the whole royal family. You can't come in those clothes, the person at the box office said, I didn't have a long skirt on, it was probably calf-length.

It was a religious piece, really lovely, I can't remember what it was called now, but it was quite, quite lovely. Anyway I said to him: I've come to Brussels from Switzerland specially for this, it was recommended to me.

Of course you can come, he says, but you'll have to wear a long skirt and be properly dressed. So I went back to the hotel, it was no further than from here to the fountain, I had another shawl with me so I put that on and went back:

et comme ça, ça va?

Yes, but what about the long skirt?

I haven't got one, I told him, and I wasn't going to go out and buy one just for one evening, when you're sitting down in the stalls you can't see anyway, I could put my shawl over my knees, there was no need for him to worry.

Après tout, vous pouvez y aller, he says to me, and how much did I pay? About 18 francs Swiss money I paid, you can work out how much that was in Belgian, for the ticket. But I didn't regret it. I had a family next to me and I kept crying: *O ça c'est beau! mmm, ça c'est bon! alors, ça on ne le trouve pas en Suisse, ça c'est magnifique!* They were so pleased for me, they came round to my hotel and asked me if I'd like to go to their house with them in their car, and we chatted about all sorts of things there, because I came from Switzerland. I could go back to Brussels again and again, it's the perfect place to visit!'

One of the best things about writing, says Gian who, when he's not painting or building something, writes faster and far more easily than I do, is that you can travel so cheaply! You start writing, he makes a sweeping motion with his hand, and you're away. He's right. I'm not really there, not at mealtimes, not in the train taking me to Bern or Zurich, or maybe even to Brussels, to the theatre. I look at the lake, the coots bob around on it like black buttons, a black line runs across the middle of the lake, darker than the chain of hills which rises up from the shore on the far side of the lake, capped with a white stripe of snow and cut mid-way across by a band of low-lying mist. It's nicer to travel if you're not writing, if you're just travelling for the sake of it, just looking out of the window for the sake of it, look, *o, ça c'est beau!* Or if you absolutely have to write, then only noting down what happens to come to mind. And what comes to mind on the train journey as we stop at one of the lakeside stations: Pablo Neruda's *Dream of the Trains.* As I look at the leafless, wintry black lilac bushes, as always when I see those bushes with their empty seed pods: *I sat down alone in the motionless train, between figures, gone away.* A girl in my school class. The only one in our class I remember. An eleven or twelve-year-old who already seemed grown up, she looked rather like a well-known poet, yes, that's how she may look today. If she still exists. One of the many girls in one of the many classes in the many schools I attended in many different places, the three different element-ary schools and three different senior schools in five different towns. *Lost souls in the trains, like keys without locks, fallen under the seat.* One single child of the four children's homes and a few other schoolmates, *perhaps they were murdered, perhaps they came back and wept.* We would no longer recognize each other, wouldn't, even if we discovered our maiden names, remember anything about each other. *A block of dead conversations.* No name and nothing else about this girl except that she was a gardener's daughter, or at least that she had a big garden at home and knew something about flowers. She said that lilac should be cut back and she brought big, heavily scented bouquets of lilac to class, bouquets I'd love now, now I haven't got a garden any more, so I could put them on the window ledge and look at the house across the way through the blossoms and leaves, like everyone else in the street does. The more you cut lilac back the stronger it will grow the following year, I remember, *in the dead smell of the journey,* in the train that goes to Biel and from there via Basel to Paris.

But Frau Gerster had already been abroad, before the war, in France. 'Staying with father's sister. She'd been married several years and didn't have any children and she came to Switzerland to visit us, and because my mother went out cleaning and washing my aunt took me in, I was able to go and stay with her in France, that was when I was three. Then war broke out and I stayed there throughout the war. And I can still remember the Germans arriving and how they didn't have ammunition left but they stayed put there, under fire. I often used to go and see them, the soldiers, the Germans, the French, the whole area, de la Marne it's called, was all mixed up. I was always getting into the trenches, and my aunt would cook potatoes and I'd fill my apron with potatoes and take them to them, they had turnips and stuff you feed animals with, that's what they ate. Now and then a soldier had some ammunition left and he'd fire. I can still remember how I used to hide myself away in the trenches with the potatoes and my aunt would have to come looking for me.

My childhood memories have always stayed with me

because I liked it so much there. In France. This sister of my father's lived about five kilometres from my grandfather in Chaumont sur Paris, Haute Marne and she was always popping over to her father's to do things for him, make the beds, do the washing up, it used to pile up, terribly untidy, because he had all this glazed crockery, a room full of it, he had a whole collection of it there and he kept bringing it out when he had a meal then someone would do the washing up and out it would all come again. And later on he sold it. And when the Germans retreated my aunt had to bring me back. She made up a little bundle, we had some embroidered material with fringes round the edges and we put my clothes into it and tied it at one corner, made a kind of little rosette, and my dolls too, anyway, she put my clothes in it and took me back to Switzerland.'

One Saturday the letter from my aunt in Switzerland arrived.

I'll be going away soon, I said at the shoemaker's where I was working: If we get our exit visas we're going to Switzerland.

A capitalist country, said one of the workers with a touch of sympathy for me, and a slightly reproachful: Do you really want to go?

Pity, said the shoemaker.

Yes, it's a pity, I said, and found it hard not to burst into tears, but I couldn't, not in front of the seven men for whom I'd been playing the grown-up for so long, and they knew I enjoyed my work, that I was happy with them and that I didn't want to go.

I spent my evenings and Sundays making knapsacks out of strips of carpet, the thick striped material which covered the stair-carpets, five large knapsacks for me, my little brother and sisters and my cousin. I made straps from the seal skins I found up in the loft with the skiing things: there are mountains in Switzerland, I thought, one day we'll be able to go skiing again. It wasn't that I didn't want to go to Switzerland. But I don't like thinking about that journey which took me away from home, I find it difficult to go on writing.

I drew the way from the house to the station later in a little leather-bound book which I'd got for my birthday and took with me. Perhaps I even started writing and drawing that very day, on the journey itself.

That drawing of us by the dike: I'm pulling the cart with the knapsacks piled up on it, my mother's out in front, the little ones and my cousin are pushing the cart and running along behind it; four trees outline the dike, the bank is a green stripe and blue lines represent the water, enough to tell me, forever, what the picture is about.

There's also a picture in the album of another departure, one with a covered waggon and a goat running after the waggon and me running after the goat and the waggon, two pictures of all the many I could have drawn and a few poems by Morgenstern written in a clumsy hand. After we got to Switzerland I tried hard for a time to stop using *Kurrent* the angular, cursive script I'd been taught to write German in at school. Unlearning other things was more difficult and there were some things I'd learnt as a child as well as a few things I'd had to learn on that journey which I couldn't shake off, although it would have been useful.

On the cloth there's an oak tree/in the shape of a person with a book. This and other poems I knew by heart when I copied them out: *Palmström doesn't dare to poke his nose in.* My grandfather had recited that to me: *He's one of those fellows/who is often suddenly, nakedly seized/by a reverence for beauty.* My grandfather was also one of those, he knew what he was teaching me. I didn't want to forget him. Unlike a lot of other things I've made up my mind to forget and then really have forgotten or as I've discovered later only thought I had forgotten. Like that journey which began in the early hours of the 1st December 1945, it was dark on the railway platform of my home town, the only lights in my picture are a thin moon and a few stars. There were no lights in the train. Now and then someone would light a cigarette, you couldn't tell if it was a Czech or a Russian soldier, if he was an enemy or a friend. I jumped at a sound my guitar made when I knocked against it accidentally. We sank back into our seats, tried to remain quiet and unnoticed all the way from Moravia to Prague, *like dead smoke in the train*, tried to steer clear of all danger.

Frau Gerster enjoys reminiscing because she enjoyed going away on holiday and she enjoyed coming home again in 1918 when the war was over:

'In Dijon, I can still see it now, it was full of Turks, they had those hats on, the ones that perch on top of their heads, red ones, Turkish hats. My aunt got me settled in a corner of the station and said she was going to go and ask about the tickets and the train. We got to Dijon without any trouble but everywhere was full of Turks, they were there to help France.'

Yes, we got to Prague without any trouble, I can see her story clear as a picture: in Prague, everywhere was full of Russians who were there, at that time, to help the Czechs.

'But my aunt didn't come back! Three days I stood there in the corner, and when I had to have a wee I just did it there in the corner behind our bundles. Then the Turkish soldiers started feeling sorry for me, I was about four and a half or five years old then, and they gave me bananas, it was the first time I'd eaten bananas, we didn't know what bananas were then, but they already had that kind of fruit in France; they brought me oranges and now and again one of them would give me some bread. They felt sorry for me and they asked me what I was doing there and I just kept saying: I'm waiting for aunty to come, so they went away and didn't take any more notice of me. My aunt had been put in prison, in a cell, they thought she was a spy. But she was lucky, one of the military guards was a cousin of hers and he recognized her and said: What are you doing in there? Of course, she burst into tears, she really howled, so he said: Hold on, I'll let you out! She came to find me, she thought I'd gone but I was still there, sitting on my bundle. I'd lost track of time, day and night went by, I slept a little here and there, then I'd wake up and eat something, I wasn't hungry, I got enough food. I remember that distinctly, that they were all Turks, I didn't see anyone else, they all had those red hats on, I remember that, yes, I think they're really lovely, like that cushion over there, that's how bright red they were.'

And where she sees hats, I see flags.

My childhood memories which are very sketchy: that I was hungry, as my brother and sisters were too, that time seemed never-ending on that journey to Prague and that from Prague to St. Margrethen it took a week, a month, or longer. But it could be that my memory is misleading me, like a clock that's wrong. But why should it be wrong. Waiting in the Swiss consulate near the castle of the Hradshin. If you go up the Nerudova Ulice, the street named after Jan Neruda, the Czech poet whose name was chosen as a nom de plume by the Chilean, Pablo Neruda, if you go up this steep street from the Nerudova the Swiss consulate is on the left, in the first building on the castle square. Here the letter with the invitation from my aunt in Zurich was endorsed and we were given travel passes for a Red Cross train which was taking foreign Swiss and concentration camp inmates and various other people like we five children to Switzerland. My memory of that square in front of the Hradshin, of the view from there, of our few hours in Prague, is like something from an illness, a high fever, I surface for a moment and become aware of my surroundings, only to sink back into sleep again immediately, dead tired.

I want to look up Jan Neruda's books in the library, he was

either born or he lived, I can't remember which now, in the street below the Hradshin, at any rate he gave it his name. But I can only find the *Kleinseitner Stories*, written a hundred years ago, which are similar to Frau Gerster's in some ways.

Yes, Dorli her daughter had already said to her: 'You should write the story of your life. And I do like reading. A man gets books for me from the library sometimes and I said to him once: You've got a lot of nonsense in that book there, there are all sorts of things in it that are true and all sorts of things that aren't, but in some places you can tell it's absolutely true, you can experience it, live it for yourself. I can see the pictures sometimes, see them in front of me, that's a special gift, no one can take that from you, that's something that's all mine, and *you* can express that for me, *you* can get that across to people, I really enjoy telling you my stories so I can give you enjoyment as well, it satisfies an inner need to be able to express yourself, to be able to write, to be able to give other people pleasure, and when you can do that you get satisfaction from your own work.

Anyway, after that she brought me back to Switzerland, my aunt did, but they only gave her half a day, she could go as far as Bern, we lived in Stöckacker then, my mother had gone to Bern in the meantime, Stöckacker is between Bern and Bümplitz. My aunt was allowed to travel on a troop train with refugees from France, it went via Pontarlier, Neuchâtel and Bern and she had to be back over the border by nightfall, I still remember that.'

We were allowed to travel on a troop train full of foreign Swiss, refugees and former concentration camp inmates from Poland and Czechoslovakia. The train went from Warsaw via Auschwitz, Prague, Hof, Munich to St. Margrethen. We got on in Prague without our mother, she had to go back and we waved from the window until she disappeared.

In Madame Serova's album there's a photograph which a sister had sent her, goodness knows how many years later. This is how I look now. Your loving Katya, is written on the card.

The Swiss soldiers took pity on us and gave us food. We were fifteen, thirteen, eight and six years old. I was allowed to help in the kitchen, in the restaurant coach and learnt how to make Maggi soup, learnt that you empty the packet into the pan first and then pour the cold water slowly onto it and then bring it to the boil, stirring all the time. At home we always said 'casserole' instead of 'pan', 'pelargonium' instead of 'geranium'. Maggi soup wasn't new to us. You could buy Maggi cubes and the thin, brown Maggi sauce where we came from, we used to like licking the sauce mix with salt off our hands. The first time I encountered Knorr and those packet soups was in Switzerland, or on that Swiss train.

And those special words which they only use in Switzerland. The soldiers on guard on the train had great fun teaching us expressions we weren't really supposed to know or were hard to pronounce like *Chuchichäschtli, Hueresaich, Potzchaib* and *Klünki* or *Glünggi.* But some Swiss wasn't entirely new to me, for as a small child I had spoken Swiss German to my Swiss grandmother and even got to understand the Zurich dialect quite well after a stay in a Swiss children's home. But this grandmother had been dead a long time by then. I had to learn everything from scratch again and the nearer we got to the Swiss border the more my Swiss German improved, but *Gopferdeckel* — I wasn't good enough for that for years.

The God-forsaken feeling at the Czech-German border, the lousy bastards might drag us off the train. Mixed feelings: they could quite easily come along, those uniformed Russians, Czechs or Germans, look at our papers, shake their heads, haul us off the train by the collar, the train would travel on to Switzerland without us and we wouldn't be saved, but at the same time, that forbidden hope that they might after all send

us back, home, that we might still be saved. Or during the
endless shunting operations that picture, wish or suspicion,
that the engine might be coupled onto the wrong end of the
train.

The desolation in Munich, the ruins around the station, I
had never seen such a wasteland before even though I had
experienced air-raids in several places. We lugged water to
the train from a tall, black pump, we got provisions for the
rest of the journey as if we really were to be travelling through
a desert.

'In a little café' a Swiss boy from Ostrau in Moravia keeps
singing, over and over again, for the entire journey the idiot
croons: 'There we sat, the two of us/with tea and cakes'. As if
all that remained to us was this nostalgic longing for tea and
cakes and love, we all hummed this one stupid tune over and
over again: 'With tea and cakes/and a little melody/played
softly.' And the people from Auschwitz smile at this, you can
see they know more than we do. Yes, unfortunately they
knew more than any of us, said Anita, whom we had adopted
as a mother. But she and Jasha keep quiet, she shows a tender
concern for us as if we were her own children, miraculously
saved, who she wanted to spare her suffering: if we had dared
to ask her she would have told us very little, as little, almost
nothing, as we had been able to get out of our father a few
months before when he returned from a German camp.

Jasha, who was young and whom I found handsome in
spite of his appalling thinness and kind in spite of his veiled
cynicism, was very attentive towards my cousin. It was
agonizing to watch him bringing her tea or soup, speaking to
her as if she were grown-up, for heaven's sake, she was only
fifteen, like me.

Something of what they were concealing, Anita, Jasha and
the others, you could see in their faces and on their bodies too,
later, when we were all disinfected in the reception camp at
the Swiss border.

Shortly before Christmas we were pronounced healthy

and clean and were released from St. Margrethen. Our knapsacks, stuffed with everything we possessed, made us look smaller than we really were, so much so that we gave my aunt, waiting for us at the station, a real fright; she told me later that she had imagined we would be bigger and not so hungry.

'And then I got covered in abscesses', says Frau Gerster: 'I must have picked something up, a virus perhaps, it spread everywhere, hands, arms, face, look here, still covered with scars, both legs covered, and there as well, and that scar used to be down there, it was open for nine years but then they massaged it up onto the cheek bone in the hospital in Langenthal. I should have had something done about it a long time ago but I couldn't, the skin had grown over the bones and they can't remove it, if they cut away at it it can fester underneath, that's when you get infections. But it doesn't really bother me, I've had it for sixty-five years, *enfin*, you can see it but no one takes any notice. In the hospital in Langenthal I had to eat porridge oats for three whole months to purify the blood, they didn't have our modern medicines then, they didn't know about penicillin, they used oats to purify the blood, oats warm you up and cleanse the system. I couldn't stand the sight of porridge for ages after that, I'm still not too keen on it. Month after month, nothing but oats morning, noon and night.'

And then we ate and ate and ate, and not just potatoes either, which we'd been having morning, noon and night, nothing but potatoes. But whole bars of chocolate, a whole one each, and whole *Ankemödeli*, which are . . . what is the word? Since then I've spoken more Swiss German than German: butter, lots of bread, my schoolfriends remember me as the girl who was always eating bread secretly in class. We devoured tarts, all the meat we could get and as we were eating my aunt, (she was a junior school teacher and not very well off) almost out of house and home and an uncle as well, we were invited by a succession of other people, who we also proceeded to alarm with our appetites.

Frau Gerster always liked travelling; later, for example, when she left school, she would have liked to go to England: 'But I already had a job then. In those days the YWCA used to look out for jobs for you, but that was out of the question for me because that's when father became ill. We had to make up for father not being able to work, so we did all sorts of things. Business wasn't good, there was a great deal of unemployment in watch-making just like there is today.'

Mademoiselle Alice assembles cog wheels on her own machine at home, all day long she sits downstairs at her machine which is new, which cost a lot of money and which she hasn't paid off yet. Or rather, she used to work. At first she hadn't noticed that the parcels of parts weren't arriving, thought the factory was still on holiday. But when she rang them to ask what was happening after waiting six weeks, she was told that there was no more work. And my machine? And my money?

'This crisis out of the blue,' says Frau Gerster: 'that's not really how it happened, they saw it coming for a long time but they didn't want to do anything about it, things would pick up again, they thought, you do get ups and downs, they thought there'd be another boom soon and no one, not the ones at the top nor the workers guessed how quickly things would change, there has to be progress, that's essential, and many's the time I myself have said: We'll get over it. These cycles, you can trace them back through the centuries when it's production and that kind of thing. It's, how should I put it, it's a way of regulating the whole world, a way of regulating surpluses, abnormal prosperity, anything that's abnormal, you only have to watch the animal world, fish, wild animals, it's all the same, when there's any over-production some disease always comes along to regulate things. It has to start all over again so it can continue. And it's the same with people, you've got the same thing with the history of man, everywhere. In my opinion everything is nicely regulated.'

All this over-production, 'these surpluses and the regulating of abnormal life': and then someone like me just stays in bed at night — 'something always comes along, like a disease, to get everything nicely regulated again.' — what's the point of working, of writing, I've had enough of this 'abnormal life' if the world is so full of books that there are more books on any one subject than anyone could ever read, this abnormal ouput, if there are whole rows of books and I can never hope to read even the most important ones, not even the ones which concern me a little. What's the point of drawing, of sculpting, the art market is saturated, the public is saturated, exhausted by whole series of names and by whole series of works which these names, these artists represent.

My enterprising grandfather, my father's father, (unlike the other one, my poetic grandfather), didn't see things like that. He, the weaver who built up his own business, couldn't have thought like that, couldn't have known. 'These cycles, when it's production and that kind of thing', in those days most people acted in good faith and were unsuspecting, it took them a long time to see what we can see now, with hindsight.

'We've been in this kind of situation before, in the past. And in those days you were just told: You've got to do your bit, which is why I couldn't go away, though I wanted to! So I went to the factory. It really was slavery, the way things used to be, the way they still are, it's always the slaves who have to start out from the bottom all over again. It always hits the weakest worst.'

She wasn't hit quite as badly as others were, said Mademoiselle Alice, because she was older, almost ready for her pension, and the rent was low and she had some savings. Others were much worse off than she was, were much poorer.

There have always been poor people here, no one else, generations of them probably, so much points to it: everything I find in this building, which is identical to the other ones in the street in its ground plan (4m. ×20m.), height and lay-out, where they've not been altered, that is. The houses on the other side of the street are only half as deep, separated from the houses at the back by a deep ditch. The windows with their little panes of glass which separate the outside rooms from the ones held captive inside and these, in turn, from the stairway, were obviously already old when they were incorporated, they're the wrong size, some of them are too big for their apertures, some are partly obstructed by a low ceiling or wall. The partitions which block off the kitchens and corridors are of rough, badly marked wooden boards with ill fitting doors, primitive handles and locks. On each floor, in a crate-like construction of this kind there's a toilet by the stairs, unheated and unventilated. And you wash in the kitchen sink.

For months now my first sight on waking has been the Rhine Falls, green glazed, above a rickety stove door and then the half-painted room. Pistachio green on ochre. Also ochre is the last of the numerous layers of paint which don't just cover the walls and ceiling of the kitchen next door but which seem actually to hold them together. Each morning I just want to pull the covers over my head and go back to sleep, I don't want to see this house again, not the old wallpaper in the cupboards, nor the cracks in the walls plugged with paper serviettes, nor the moths. Nor smell the smell of the cupboards, the smell which our clothes are absorbing, which gets worse every day and which you can't get rid of by washing or airing. Nor the old lady's bits and pieces which we're forever throwing away, yet which are always turning up again. Not to have to face the delapidation by which I am surrounded, which gets on my nerves, everyone's nerves. This house is like the houses in my bad dreams, a constant process of decay, it's not like the house I dreamed of for myself, that was going to be a bright modern house.

'God rewards the diligent', was painted on a ceramic plate we were given by an old lady as a wedding present; I can imagine Frau Gerster giving wedding presents like that. We put the plate away so we couldn't see the motto any more. Consider the lilies of the field how they grow; they toil not neither do they spin, we thought, because we lack a certain sense of discipline.

And Frau Gerster too thinks 'It's always the ones who lack a certain discipline, who've only managed to get part of the way, to a certain stage, who feel it first, it hits the poor first. Why? The others are clever, the other kind of person is. And the ones at the top certainly are, the ones at the top help each other out, they've got so far, they've got a certain footing: We're staying here, we're not slipping down! And so it's the ones at the bottom who are hit. The ones in the middle get hit too but not the more experienced ones, it doesn't matter what kind of experience they've got, they know how to look after themselves.

Anyway, father was unemployed. If I can't get any work we'll start our own business, he said when they came from Stöckacker and he didn't have any work and mother had some money from the family. The shop next door which had been a grocer's was for sale. They went to see it and bought it. And it went quite well. They started to sell vegetables, father used to ride on his bike across the big moor.'

The big moor, I know it a little. I went round looking for a flat on a bicycle I hired at the station at Ins. I happily cycled the length and breadth of the big moor, through the villages alongside the Murtensee. At the wayside inns men sat drinking white wine and wondering why I should want to live in these parts, how should we live, after all, you need money to live. *O les artistes!* They were artists too! they laugh. See! It's Wednesday morning and we're sitting here drinking wine! And I'm sent from one person to the next: Perhaps there's a flat free there, or an empty barn somewhere else, they promise to help me in my search and take down my address.

The area seemed familiar right from the start: the straight roads cutting across the wide plain, the tree-lined paths which divide the fields up into enormous units, ancient avenues and narrow tracks leading up to tall buildings, too big for farmhouses, to prisons. Much, a great deal, reminded me of the Moravian plain which I often cycled across, above Olomuc where I come from.

'Father used to cycle across the big moor to get eggs and fruit and vegetables, one big basket at the front and another at the back, on the carrier, that's what we sold. Groceries and liqueurs as well and wine, that was still sold by the measure then, we had a cask with a tap in the shop and you poured out a litre or half a litre, people used to come for three decilitres or two or one decilitre, I still remember all about that, we had these glasses or bottles for up to five litres. We had foreign wines as well, French wine, cognac, that came in barrels. We had to dilute the cognac ourselves. It was ninety percent proof when it arrived and it had to be reduced to forty-eight, that was the law. You had to boil water for quite a long time, let it stand and then pour it in really slowly, that's how it was done. And we sold cheese, Italian cheese, Gorgonzola, that was our speciality. We had everything, special cheeses, mortadella, salami, all kinds of things the butchers didn't have in those days, it was a specialist shop. A bank bought the building later, it belonged to a company and we had to get out and this place was for sale and mother got some more money, inherited it, so we bought it, we've been here since 1921. It was a good buy, we were able to put down a big deposit and didn't pay much interest, we managed fine, but then father became ill. In the end he needed two sticks to get about. They didn't know about arthrosis, sclerosis and that sort of thing in those days, but father probably had arthrosis, both his legs were paralysed, both his hips completely paralysed, I must have inherited some of it otherwise I wouldn't have had the operation for arthrosis. Father became an invalid and you just had to be able to fend for yourself, you had to work to help make ends meet, you had to help bring in the money, mother always worked, we did everything for ourselves, that's been the story of my life. I had to do everything in the shop because father was so weak and I was so strong. I humped bags of sugar, everything; sugar didn't come in little packets then you know, or maybe the cube sugar did, it was delivered in big boxes. We had the shop until '38 but I left in '31, I went to work in Biel and then I met my husband there and we got married in '32.

I've just got one sister, she's twenty-one months older than me. She always lived at home.'

I don't know how old the girl next door is, the one who has to stay in the house all day, who only gets to go out shopping with her mother once in a while, in the evening. There aren't many people in the shop then and her mother can be almost certain that she won't spit at anyone. She might be fourteen, maybe even sixteen. I've tried to have a word with her a few times as I've gone past, I've called *'ciao'* up to her; she's stayed at the window, looking at me, propped on her elbows, watching. Once when I saw her observing me as I tried to move the handle of the front door with one hand while clutching a bulging carrier bag with the other one, I threw her a mandarin, which she caught.

Always in the house. Does she also defend herself against the washing-up, the ironing, the vacuuming by spitting? The girl must also have spat at school, the day must have come when she didn't like the teacher or the teacher didn't like her, so she had to defend herself. Maybe spitting was all she had left, spitting was her way of revolting. She doesn't have to learn or work or earn money, staying at home has become her way of life.

Frau Gerster met her husband at the sports factory: 'I worked upstairs and he was downstairs, there were about four of us, good workers. It's quite funny the way it happened, he carried a crate in one day, brought it in for us, and I shut the door in his face, right in his face, but I opened it for him right away and he said: You damned fool!, just joking, like: Little idiot! It didn't take long after that. He was engaged, he had been engaged to someone for about nine months and then they quarrelled and of course he sent her the ring back. Then, one Sunday morning, there he was, ringing the bell: I've come to see you. Probably wanted to see what our home was like. He was never one for a lot of words, he just acted. He had one brother who was a boxer. He lost a lot of blood, Paul did, when he was boxing, I think I've already told you about him, he lost too much blood boxing and the white blood cells multiplied more than the red ones and he became ill. He had this brother and a mother, I had seen her once on the station square, and not much money, that's why he was on piece-work at that time. I often used to go out with him for something to eat, but because he earned next to nothing and sometimes the work was really lousy, I said to him: listen, we've got plenty of fruit and stuff going rotten at home. So I'd bring him a big piece of bread or some fruit or I'd sneak some salami or mortadella and make him sandwiches. I helped him as much as I could, I've always liked helping people.

Just like with Karl, I was always good to him, five whole years I fed him and gave him money, it was like a home from home for him here, his mother knew he was doing as he was told, she used to say to me: I'm so happy he can be with you! And now she's got a completely different story. It's all gone wrong.

Of course, there are a lot of people who accept help when they don't need it and there are the others who do need it but who don't say anything, and that's good. That's honourable, that shows a noble character, that's what you don't find with well-off people. There are plenty of people prepared to use you, while the ones who really need help don't show they need it and if you give them something it's very rewarding, you can tell immediately if someone's suffering, you can tell, it's easy.'

Helping. No, we shouldn't just walk past the spitting girl next door like we do, 'if someone's suffering you can tell, it's easy.' I ought to find out more about her.

Maybe you should learn to spit for her sake, use it as a common language, a means of communication, maybe you should organize spitting competitions, or just do as actors do, spitting over their shoulders for luck before the performance to ward off evil spirits. Maybe you should learn to spit boldly, that shouldn't be difficult for me, I could do it well enough when I was little, three or four years old. I used to spit all my food out in those days, I used to bring everything up. I can't remember now what I was trying to defend myself against, I only know it didn't do any good. I wasn't locked in but I was sent to a children's home and when I didn't stop doing it there I was sent to another one and then another one. I really should learn to help myself before I can be of more help to others.

One time, when Frau Gerster still had her dog and she was walking along the street with him: 'This old man came towards me and his face was all grazed and covered in blood, so I shouted out: Pépé, that's an expression they use in the Vaud, Pépé, and he came over to me and I asked him what had happened. And he told me he'd been up in Bern and had got into an argument with someone in the station buffet and in his fury he just kept drinking and he couldn't take it. Anyway, he had fallen over and scraped his face. Then, as he's walking up the street, he says to me: I'm going into that bar over there, and I say: No, you musn't do that, you must go straight home! Look at your face! But he insisted he had to go to the bar. Then a worker from the building site came along and I said to him: I'm taking him home, you come with me. So we took him up to his place, laid him on a bed and tried to undress him. Don't mind me, I told him, I do know what a man looks like, and the chap who helped me with him was a man, a father, I told him, we were just going to put him to bed. But he didn't want us to. And his wife was blind. He told her to make some coffee. It didn't occur to me that she was blind, I hadn't noticed anything, but then there was the way she kept so close to the wall when she went into the kitchen, so I said: Pépé, you just keep quiet now, I'll make some coffee, and I went out to the kitchen. She said I was to make sure she didn't do anything wrong and she made the coffee herself, but when I'd seen where she kept everything I gave her a hand and she insisted that we had our coffee in the other room. So I laid the table, carried the cups through, helped her.'

I can see Pépé's blind wife, and her flat.

All the objects left behind by Madame Serova: the red enamelled vase with its plastic flowers embedded in sand, a plastic flowerpot on a shelf, high up in one of the dark corners of the room, the patched lace curtains between the inner and outer windows and the Chinese flowered plastic covering on the firewood chest and the table, four layers thick, and on the little window in the kitchen door, and the flowered cups held together with wire — all this, everything around me forces my thoughts back to the old emigrée. The way she gropes her way around the flat, muttering, supporting herself on the table, the wood chest, a duster in her hand, not blind but, as Frau Gerster says: without a language, one of the foreigners who have no language. And all of this forces me to imagine living here without the power to change anything.

'And Pépé sobered up the more coffee we drank, he had an empty stomach so the alcohol had had a strong effect. Now you must get some food inside you! And it was then she told me they wanted to go into a home and had tried everywhere with no luck. So of course I said I'd go right away and make sure they got in somewhere, as long as they weren't going to go and change their minds! I went along to the town hall, I banged on the desk and really let them have it. I said: Surely this is what you're here for, isn't it? These people have told you they want to go into a home. They said they didn't have any vacancies. If you can find room for other people then you must be able to find room for them. Shall we see what we can do or shall I take it higher up? That got things going and two days later they were told they could move into an old people's home and that's where they are to this day.

Their children never came to see them, but when it came to dividing up the belongings they turned up all right. I left it all to the welfare people, that was their job.'

Madame Serova's old hand-made silk dresses and kimonos, her Chinese cushions with brightly coloured dragons, the white enamel pots and pans with Chinese writing underneath, the photograph album — there's a lot there to help me reconstruct the story of her life. The flight from Russia, (her friend, my neighbour who is also from Rusia, knows the name of the place), Hong Kong, the journey here, her life here after her husband's death when she hardly ever left the house, hardly ever spoke to anyone. I understand the refugees' desire to be untraceable, to be safe from persecution.

And since I've been here this state of mind has returned to me, I feel a similar sense of relief, of liberation: no one knows our address, our telephone number, only a handful of our closest friends know that we have moved from our old home.

Now, two years on, things aren't like that any more.

But I'm not going to write the story of Madame Serova's life, or not yet, I'm going to guard against identifying with her while we're still doing our alterations here.

For we seem to be in constant danger of failing in our attempt to change, in our attempt to create a new lifestyle for ourselves here.

When Gian tears down one of the wooden boardings which divide up the interior of the flat into corridor, dining room and store room, part of the plaster ceiling falls to the floor together with all the rubbish from the cavity above, so that the floor looks as if it's going to give way any minute because of the weight, and the plaster on the ceiling below that cracks and falls off in great pieces: piles of rubbish everywhere, on the top floor, in the kitchen, in the corridor, on the stairs, in our hallway, in front of the loo door, in the loo itself, (which is hardly fit to be used), on the lower part of the staircase, rubbish, all of which has to be carried in buckets down the steep steps and taken away. A quite impossible undertaking, it seems to me, at any rate it's more than one man can manage. And I can't help Gian carry the buckets, at the first attempt my back goes on strike and forces me to become a spectator. How the dust trickles through the cracks in the ceiling. With a cloth, with Madame Serova's duster, I go round her flat, our flat, wiping dust from the window sills, from the table, from the stove, from the edges of the cupboard, the doors, the sideboard, from the glass cupboard above the sink, I shake it out of the beds, brush it out of my hair and clothes, out of the children's hair and clothes. The dust doesn't just settle *on* everything, ears, the corners of my eyes, mouth, it seems to have penetrated right *into* me, through my nose and mouth, through the pores of my skin, as if I'm all dusty inside.

Gian carries two heavy buckets of rubble down the stairs, two floors, three flights of narrow, winding, worn wooden stairs, hour after hour, day after day, singing at first then, towards evening, night, swearing. His hair stands up, stiff and grey with dust, eyelashes and beard stubble dusty-grey. Only his eyes are their usual brown, and I can see him singing and swearing as he used to do at school.

'Where were we?' asks Frau Gerster: 'Oh yes, cuddling! Anyway, he came and rang the bell. I dashed downstairs in my dressing gown, grumbling away to myself: This is a sorry state of affairs when a person can't even have a lie-in of a Sunday morning! I thought it was someone coming to the shop, you see. The shop was open every day from seven until about ten at night, no lunch break either, not like it is today, no Wednesdays and Saturdays free, so I grumbled away: A sorry state of affairs it is when you have to be at people's beck and call even on a Sunday, and they'll want credit as well if you'll give it to them, and what happens then? You have to go running round trying to get the money out of them — all down the corridor, all down the stairs I was grumbling away like this, and he could hear me outside, we didn't have the double door then. And he started to laugh. So I opened the door and of course all the wind went out of my sails, there I was standing in my dressing gown, absolutely dumbfounded. I said: What on earth are you doing here!

I've come to see you, he said.

Are you mad? What's come over you? I said, I must go and put some clothes on.

As you like, he said: I'll come in with you, I'm not embarrassed, I've got sisters of my own.

I got dressed and he went in to see my parents and we all sat round talking. But he didn't mention that he'd broken off his engagement, he didn't say anything about it, I've just come to have a look, he told my parents, I was just curious to see what

Bethli's home was like. Then we made a date and I went along, and when we were working together he'd sometimes walk me to the station and one thing led to another until we started cuddling. It all happened in nine months, we were cuddling for nine months, it began in September, we got engaged in December and we were married in March.

He'd been going out with another girl for five months before that, engaged, but it didn't work out. His fiancée's mother was a fortune-teller and he wasn't very happy about that. So he said to me: That's it. Now I've seen what's what I want to get married, he was twenty-eight, your parents can say what they like but I want to get married now! I want you and no one else!

So I said: And don't you mind me being so fat? Of course not, I'd rather have a nice, good-natured fatty than some underfed bag of bones!'.

And don't you mind me being so thin? I wonder, I used to wonder. But no, deer and gazelles aren't fat either, Gian said he didn't like fat girls.

'He came straight out with it! Then one thing led to another and we got married.

I'd been terribly ill just before, in November, with bronchial pneumonia. He often came to visit me at home. I was in a pretty bad state, he'd found me unconscious in bed two or three times, my mother was out at work, my sister too, so he came up to the second floor where my sister and I slept and when he'd found me like that two or three times he said: That's enough, I'm taking you with me, he got angry: you're coming home to me. My mother's at home all day, she doesn't know what to do with herself, she's got plenty of time to look after you. And then I had a row with mother. As I've said, you should never be rude to people but she did get pretty nasty with me, of course it was all rather a shock for her, with father being ill my money did make a difference. But I said: I'm

going. I'll be well looked after there. I remember it clearly, it
was a Saturday and on the Sunday morning they had to get
the doctor to come. My husband got told off afterwards by his
brother for bringing such a sickly creature home, he told him
to think carefully about what he was doing. On the Sunday
morning Dr. Maurer came at eleven and said I might have a
pulmonary haemorrhage or an embolism, I was in a very poor
state but he'd do all he could for me. He came again at two and
then at six and at ten. His brother wasn't very pleased about all
this: Are you crazy, he said; her parents could have you up
before the courts for just taking the girl like that. But he said:
For God's sake! I love her! I can't just leave her there in that
state!'

We were at the same school for a year, it was my first year at
the school and his last. Like many of the pupils I travelled in
from Wollishofen by train and for months I watched him
waiting at the end of the platform for his girlfriend and then
walking to school with her, through the grounds of the
Museum, through the park which lies between the Limmat
and the Sihl, across the little iron bridge, and then back again
in the afternoon. I longed to have such a faithful friend myself
one day.

   Sometimes he looks over my shoulder while I'm modelling,
bends over me and watches my battle with two figures, trying
to bring their limbs round to form a circle. He doesn't say
much, but suddenly the limbs, the figures, the whole work
falls into place. A really arrogant fellow, says Jonel from my
class as Gian goes out of the door. Why does that hurt? He
pushes my bicycle along the Bahnhofstrasse, I walk beside
him, look at him from the side, listening as he talks. What did
we say to each other? *Tschapatalpis*! A term of endearment?
Puppy! Lusty young dog! Is that supposed to be a compliment?
Sniff.

   As a farewell when he left school, we, his school friends,

went up to the Uetliberg, he had one girlfriend on his right and one on his left and one in front; I without any hesitation sought to count myself among the girlfriends and walk beside him. But where was my place? When you've already got one on your right and on your left and at your feet . . . for I was cheeky and full of high spirits, I thought I deserved a good time after everything I'd been through, and that made him so . . .

have things gone so far that I'm starting to tell anecdotes, because of Frau Gerster? Spinning yarns from my desires, my joys, my celebrations, my fun?

Frau Gerster got engaged that Christmas: 'It was Christmas day when I got up for the first time at their house and we decided to get engaged straight away. The doctor said: When you get up, try some walks together in the woods, for the air. There'd been quite a lot of snow, I put some high boots on, they wrapped another shawl round me so I wouldn't catch cold, his mother took one arm and he took the other, so I'd stay on my feet and we walked up into the woods, it did me a world of good. And come New Year he said: What shall we do for New Year? So I said: I'd give anything to hear a really good *Ländler* band! And just as if I'd divined it, sure enough there was a good *Ländler* band playing at the station restaurant in Brügg. So he says: Come on then, we'll go and see what it's like, you've been out of bed a week now, I pulled round fast once I was up and I put the woollen *Gloschli* on — a kind of petticoat, I put that on and then I wanted to dance. Do you think you should? What about your heart? Oh, I don't care, say I, if I'm going to die I might as well die here as in bed, right now I want to have some fun! And that's what he liked about me, among other things, I was lively, really lively when I was young. So we went dancing. New Year's Eve, New Year's Day, the band moved on to Busswil on New Year's Day and we went with it. On St. Berzelius' Day, on the second of January, we went out dancing again, all day. Sunday was New

Year's Day, Monday was the second of January and of course by Tuesday I was tired so I went to bed for a while and his mother started lecturing me: I'd been irresponsible, she'd been terribly worried. So I say to her: I'm fit now, that's what matters, isn't it? On Thursday I had to go to the doctor's and he said: What have you been doing? Something had happened, had I been to some quack doctor? No, but I can't tell you. He says: I want to know what you've been up to! All right, I went out dancing on New Year's Eve, New Year and St. Berzelius' Day, but I had a woollen petticoat on, look, there it was, and he just had to laugh at that, he was an older doctor, the most senior one at the Inselklinik in Bern. I sweated it out, the pneumonia, I literally danced it out of me. Just before we got to the dance hall I'd take the petticoat off so I didn't sweat too much and when we left I'd put it on again, I was forever changing, I always had the petticoat with me in my bag and that's what did the trick. Anyway, he said I should go to Beatenberg for a cure, two or three weeks perhaps. But I said to him: If I'm fit again I'm going back to work and I didn't go for a cure, I went back to work and I was fine. I didn't have pneumonia or anything of that kind for a long time afterwards. But Maurer, Dr. Maurer said to me: You've got a strong constitution, you must have been healthy in the first place to have come through it, to have recovered so well! And he said to my mother-in-law: That's a good wife your son's getting, she's very healthy, she'll be able to cope with anything, she's tough, solid, sturdy!'

That old longing for someone who, even when at the same school, was always far away. I remember the few occasions when we came closer, but was he really any nearer then, nearer than in my thoughts? When I was furthest away, my longing already almost forgotten, I was actually closest to him. Would he have written otherwise? And every time I go away it's just the same, even now.

In Mamaroneck, N.Y., we sat in front of the television, my two younger sisters, my little brother and I were watching 'Swiss Family Robinson', in English: all the Robinson family's adventures in the jungles of New Guinea, adventures for me, just the kind I liked, the kind I wanted to have myself. One of the first things we bought when we arrived in the States was this television set, it was supposed to help us learn the language, learn American as quickly as possible from westerns, advertisements, politics, detective series, become Americans as quickly as possible. The shipwreck and the taming of the ostrich and most of all the wonderful tree house in New Guinea, I can still see it all: my dream house, the one I had built as a child in an old tree in our garden, which wasn't nearly as good as the one the Robinson family built. The wide platform on the first level with all the different entrances, the windows cut into the thick trunk which also held the stairway, while I had to climb an ordinary piece of rope to reach the wobbly raised hide. I worked at it a whole summer, heaved building materials up into the great oak tree, covered the framework of boughs with a tarpaulin and filled in the walls with box lids and sacking until I could sit and read in my own little house, undisturbed by my brother and sisters. I even spent a night there eventually, the wind howled and the rain disturbed me a little.

As I sit before the perfect tree house the postman brings a letter, wrongly addressed, which has arrived in the right street in the right part of New York after a round-about six week journey from Switzerland, from the Engadine. I know the handwriting, a snow-grouse feather falls from the opened envelope, floats white to the floor in front of the flickering jungle. No need to read what Gian has written.

That letter was addressed to the right person, she had been working in New York for nearly two years, had had quite different adventures in a different kind of jungle, and she hadn't gone under, 'she'll be able to cope with anything, she's tough, sturdy', even if she doesn't look it.

The Gersters announced their engagement on the fourth of January. 'Then I had to wait ten weeks for the papers because I was still an Italian then, we were all Italians even though we were born in Switzerland because father was Italian, although he'd never been there either, except when he went to get the papers for his marriage.'

Then I had to wait months for my papers, they were in some office somewhere in Czechoslovakia which seemed to ignore my enquiries.

I came back to Switzerland in February via Le Havre and Paris, Gian came to meet me there, 'we cuddled, nature, that was our joy', until July, in Val Bever, in Val Roseg and in the beautiful woods behind Alp Prüma. Then the authorities made an exception and gave me permission to marry so we didn't become too much of a worry to my grandmother, Gian's parents and the kind people we were renting a room from.

'So we got married.

His brother came to the wedding and died soon afterwards. A year later, not quite a year, we were married in the March and by that autumn he was confined to bed, we were with him at Christmas, New Year, that's when we went up to Zweisimmental for the first time. At the hospital they told him it was to do with his white blood cells, they didn't realize then that it was leukaemia or something like it, they gave him gold injections to boost the red blood cells, we paid for those. Every time he had one of those injection we got a bill for sixty-five francs, I've still got them, he had six gold injections all in all and we paid each bill as it came so it didn't mount up. They managed to get his blood back up to eighty-eight percent of the normal count and they let him go home, but they did tell him that he wasn't to . . . that on no account was he to sleep with a woman, no intercourse at all or that would be it. Anyway, at that time there was a woman living on the same floor as him, next door, a divorcée, a real picture! When he came home she fairly captivated the poor boy, he was a good-looker as well, and she slept with him. Not long after that we had to take him back because the white cells had started to multiply again, he ate too little, what they gave him wasn't that good anyway and he just didn't feel like it, and as time went by he got steadily more and more tired until he was in a terrible state and I went to Bern with him and they said everything was all arranged and that I should go back to Zweisimmental with him so he could convalesce. On Christmas Day we got the message asking us to go to my brother-in-law right away, he wasn't at all well, and when we got there, I can still see him, he had a little bird on the bed and he said to me: Look what a good friend I've got, Bethli. And he didn't say a word about the lady or about Oberstock where he'd been with her or what had happened there. He fed the bird and it came into the room on his finger. So I said: How marvellous, such a lovely friend.

Paul looks terrible, you know, I said to my husband, I don't like the look of him. The doctor said it could happen suddenly, any time. When we left he was pretty bad and then on New Year's Eve there was a telephone call to say he'd died, he'd got an infection, meningitis. The lady stayed with him and then she also died, about three months later, but she stayed with him right to the end, she sat with him so at least he had somebody there and I was pleased he had someone with him. We went up there again and he was buried in Zweisimmental.

It's strange, when I go into the mountains I always lose weight, all I have to do is go into the mountains. In Leysin, after my operation I lost five kilos in the first week and they got worried and said it wouldn't do. But I was still eating the same as usual. Then my weight went up again quite suddenly, it's the amount of oxygen I'm taking in, that's what it is. I put on weight again as they wanted, slowly, a pound a week, until

I got back to my old weight and since I left there my weight has never altered. I can be ill, it doesn't make any difference what kind of state I'm in, I'm always fine when my weight is up.

And I'm going out for walks again now. I couldn't go out the same as usual last winter because I got pyelitis and then I got 'flu on top of that, I'm getting about again now but I can't go as far as I used to. Of course, you mustn't forget I've still got my operations, they're still there, three operations all in all, they told me at the hospital I'd have to be careful. That was two years ago and it's started to ease up now, I'm slowly getting back to normal. Maybe I haven't got enough confidence in myself, although I thought I had, I can't say I'm not strong, either, *confiance*, that's what you call it, it's a matter of confidence in my own body, in my own health, I'm always afraid something could go wrong again and until I can get rid of that fear I won't be a hundred percent fit. That's the first thing they told me at the hospital, I shouldn't try to lose weight, no dieting. I've always been bonny, I've been fat since I was a baby, but my husband didn't mind, a fat, good-natured kind of person was all right by him.'

We sat my grandmother and Gian's great aunt in a carriage and went merrily up into the mountains, to Fex where we got married. The priest talked of our future, of the enterprise we would work together to establish, hand in hand we would work at creating what parents and priests think a young couple should create. We ourselves had very different ideas about our future, had never imagined having this kind of wedding, and we proceeded to abandon anything the moment it threatened to become an 'enterprise', any work that started coming too easily, and swapped it for something which was much more of a challenge. Looking back, especially when I look at our five children, I'm amazed, or rather horrified, at all the risks we took.

'Anyway, I invited her to the wedding, mother, but she didn't come. She didn't speak to me for a long time. My sister acted as a witness. And his brother was also there. Father couldn't come because of his legs, he could only get about on two sticks then.

Mother and I made it up later. She came round one day, father had been angry with her, had hit her, he'd had too much to drink in the pub opposite and had come home in a bad mood. She says: I'm never going back there again. But I'm out all day mother, what are you going to do? But the landlady next door is ill, she's gone to Zweisimmental, maybe you could look after the house for her, she's got three children, that might be a possibility, then you'd be here, I don't mind. The lady took in boarders when they were building the new canal lock at Nidau and her eldest daughter did the housework during the holidays. When it was time for her to go away again my mother took over. She had to cook for the boarders, she was there a good two, three months. And while she was there father went to see her a few times, said she ought to come home, hadn't she had enough yet, so I gave him a talking to. Then mother went home, but she got a job in the same factory as my sister. Father was on his own at home all day, she always made his dinner for him when she came home.'

The success of an expedition often depends on the quality of the food, we were told by a friend who had just returned from an expedition to the South Pole. If the meals were boring or plain bad the morale of the members of the expedition, who were under a great deal of stress anyway, would sink visibly. Gian is under a great deal of stress now, we all are. Luckily I find it great fun cooking on the little wood-fired stove which the Spaniards left standing upstairs and which we carried down into Madame Serova's kitchen. And shopping here is also a pleasure, would be a pleasure if only I found it easier to get out of the house. The shops are all quite near, the baker's, the dairy round the corner, vegetables and groceries, *comestibles* as they're called here, the butcher's, little, old shops for the most part.

All I can do is cook as best I can. The wood I'm using for the stove was chopped by Madame Serova, her chopping block, all eaten by woodworm, is in the cellar next to the pile of firewood. The chippings, the small pieces of firewood and the twigs, together with the Russian newspapers are in a big wooden chest in the kitchen.

Fiftieth anniversary of the presentation of Leo Tolstoy's estate, 'Yasnaya Polyana' to the Soviet people. Had Madame Serova read the NOVOYE RUSSKOYE SLOVO of the twenty-second of August 1971, had she really read this article? *Although the condition of the estate leaves somthing to be desired, it welcomes thousands of visitors each year, visitors who are gripped by the poetic spirit of the house, now a museum, and the other buildings, as well as the tree-lined avenues and the poet's favourite seat in the surrounding parkland.* It was even more pompous in the original, writes Eliette, who has taken the paper and translated it for me. (Eliette, one of my book characters, my literary model who's been frightened away by Frau Gerster. She can speak Russian.) There's nothing to indicate that Madame Serova was interested in Tolstoy or his estate, but thousands are gripped by the poetic spirit there, nevertheless. Perhaps she read about the reappearance of Shakovsky in the edition dated the 28. 8. 70, MOSCOW DISCUSSIONS ABOUT IMMORTALITY and FRESH SAUSAGES *from our sausage factory, visit our factory and see the quality and freshness for yourself!* Fresh Russian sausages in the USA. For the paper is printed in New York, 243 West 56th Street, and it arrives here via an address in Richmond, ME., — the address of relatives, or friends?

I can paint over the wall paper, which I suppose Madame

Serova liked, and when the paint dries and to my annoyance the flower pattern still shows through, I can give it another coat or I can rip it off and paint the room white, but that also presents problems because there are patches which blister, where the paint peels off and other patches where the wall paper simply will not come away, not with all my scraping. There's always fresh dirt to be swept off the floor, dust to be dusted.

One of us should earn some money pretty quickly. I can teach a German class once a week in Biel.

I'm trying to put together for the Association of Swiss Architects some of the observations I've made here while we've been building. But what I find easy to write for my diary, just for me, becomes a struggle when it's to be something useful, something for other people to read, something I can make some money from.

I have a commission to illustrate a book. But all I can do is cook, clean, wash, dust. I've got too little self-confidence. *Confiance.*

Remains have built up like a geological strata under years of thick dust, remains left by generations of tenants, things which were no longer of use, things forgotten at moving time but which for one reason or another, maybe from laziness or thrift, were never thrown away.

Gian carries loads of stove-pipes, mattresses with their striped covers ripped and the horsehair and woollen stuffing spilling out. He has to hump countless numbers of these stained, torn mattresses with their springs poking through the covers down the stairs, as well as iron bedsteads and old gas stoves. With *confiance* in his own strength Gian removes the old wiring, the partitioning in the loft, carefully replaces the rotten floorboards, a supporting beam, with Patrick's help, father and son replace the attic stairs. At the height of the summer heat they insulate the roof with glass wool and aluminium foil and insert a strip of fibreglass as a skylight. Using the old rope winch, the kind you can see fixed on every roof here, we heave a bath up to the top of the building, an event which attracts quite a gathering of onlookers in the street below. Careful, I shout, *attention!* Would the children move to one side because we can't be sure that the rope or the roof beam which holds the pulley will take the weight, *attenzione!* But the children stay there, watching open-mouthed. I can't speak Spanish, so I call to the watching mothers to help.

To go with the bath there's an old-fashioned washbasin which we found in a box under a pile of rubbish in the attic. There was also a metal hairdryer and some other hairdressing equipment, a hairdresser must have lived and worked here once, and a shoemaker whose stool, hammer and various other tools were the only things, out of all the rubbish here, that we could make use of, apart from the washbasin. Perhaps we could also have used the purple settee, carefully covered with newspaper, THE NEW RUSSIAN WORD, but the flat is too full, we've got all the building materials stored in here as well as our furniture. We could offer the settee to Frau Gerster or her sister.

'No', they say, 'no thank you.' They've got complete suites of furniture. Yes, her sister, too. 'Because my sister got married in the meantime, she was really taken for a ride, she didn't have to get married at all. He promised her all sorts of things but nothing came of any of it. Three days after their wedding this fellow says to her: Don't think I married you just so I'd have to go to work to keep you, you can go out to work yourself. I'm staying in bed! And he even thought that my father, who was an invalid, should bring him his breakfast in bed! They lived apart for three months, she stayed with me, and then she got a divorce, she got it in about three hours, the divorce that is, they could see that it wasn't quite . . . anyway, all in all the marriage lasted six months. She's always worked, forty-six years in the same factory. Until New Year the year before last. Putting grain and matt finishes on with brushes, that was her speciality, you can get gold bowls, clock cases which aren't shiny, which are matt, that's what she did.'

We often come close to regretting how careful we've always been to preserve something that's taken our fancy, even if it's not an antique, not anything of particular value. And time and time again some well-meaning person comes along and explains how to do something the right way, explains that it should be done differently, and he can never understand that we don't want change just for the sake of it, not just to make something look better, that we only want change when it's really necessary. We need a bath, water pipes which the water will flow along properly rather than pouring down the outside as it does now, we need a heating system which doesn't smoke. But we don't need a flat to show who and what we are (although this is probably unavoidable in the long run), and we don't want to set up a memorial to ourselves. The way it looks at the moment, that would be a joke.

We just want to satisfy our own requirements and our work-plan entails rebuilding with the old bricks, re-utilizing building materials which still bear the traces of previous occupants, using the rough boards of the kitchen and hall partitioning for the loft extension and the old battens for folding doors, in two layers with a sheet of plastic stretched over them, refitting the shabby old doorframes and doors.

Just wanting to satisfy our own requirements. With our conversion, that is. As if it were as easy to apply that principle to our other work, Gian's and mine, to our life stories, as Frau Gerster says. As if satisfying your own requirements was easy. Even if, occasionally, I have been lucky enough (if that's what you call it) to accomplish a picture, a good figure, a good piece of writing. As if it were possible to dream the same dream twice or to dream endless numbers of new dreams.

How is this going to be concealed, asks the electrician who is checking the storage heaters we've made, and he shakes his head when he notices that you can see the aluminium foil under the roof insulation.

The electrician, *le patron*, shakes his head pityingly at the white-painted Novopan tiles on the floor of the studio and one of its walls, which used to be the kitchen wall and which had at one stage been painted by a naive Mondrian blue, black-brown and white. But then he wouldn't approve of a genuine Mondrian or Miró. Why should he? He starts to sketch his wiring plan onto the freshly whitewashed walls and launches into a lengthy explanation of the correct way of going about an alteration of this kind. But then you have to bring in the professionals, he says and perhaps he realizes people like us cannot afford that.

Even the man from southern Italy who has come round in the evenings to help us remove the crumbling plasterwork and resurface the walls thinks it's a shame that we're not covering them with plasterboard. His own flat is feudal, or bourgeois, and he simply cannot understand all the trouble we're going to.

Mademoiselle Alice shakes her head: Those blue window frames in the children's room, do you like them? And she too insists that the distempered walls should have been given a coat of gloss paint: If you don't want them shiny, though that's much more practical, there's always matt paint. And the kitchen walls simply have to be painted properly, you can't use distemper there, a neighbour of hers whose kitchen walls are distempered has to have them repainted every few months, every time a tenant, a paying-guest leaves. Suddenly angry at our unwillingness to take her advice, Mademoiselle Alice paints the rest of her flat pale green and apricot, gloss paint. She loves pale green, mignonette, so relaxing.

Even the outside of the building is pale green, the owner and most of the tenants seem to love pale green. Personally the colour and the shine of the paint in my room remind me of pistachio ice cream which I always choose when I have ice cream, because of the colour, or rather because of a childhood memory.

But it's not just the pistachio green around me that makes me think of Italy, of secret night-time outings in Riccione. The girl who was supposed to be looking after us used to take us along when she had a rendez-vous, probably for protection as much as anything else. Ten o'clock in the evening, inwardly triumphant, we sat at marble tables on the pavement around a lantern and little Martini or Cinzano bottles, in our light summer clothes, it was so warm, conspirators.

The noise too which rises up from the street, all the voices and the singing, all this makes me think of Italy. Not of the enormous thick stone bath tub in a round stone building which, we were told, was the coffin, the sarcophagus of a king and not his bath tub, pity, no, rather it makes me think of hot evenings, the sort we can get here too sometimes, of tired, almost unbearable days on the beach, and the smell also, as if the Adriatic were just around the corner, the water stinking in the heat, the water which for us is the lake. I'd love to go for a swim now.

We could row out to the middle of the lake where it's not so dirty, dive into the water and let it wash away the dust and sweat.

'They always say they shouldn't go swimming,' says Frau Gerster, 'but when he'd been in the lake I always took him to the fountain and gave him a good shower. The lake is very dangerous for dogs, it's nice for them to have the water but you really should wash them afterwards otherwise they'll get eczema. Not just with anything. You have to use a dog shampoo, it doesn't dry the skin and they'll have a healthy coat then. Lots of brushing too, especially the long-haired ones, you have to brush them a lot, there's no getting away from it. Oh yes, I've seen lots of things in my time, down by the lake, but I've got no *fiduz* left for the lake, not like I used to have. No *fiduz* means there's no pull there, no attraction any more, no interest. It can also mean you don't like going on the lake any more, or that you've lost your interest in travel. You can say no *fiduz* to that as well.'

No, I haven't got any *fiduz* left for travelling either, it's gone, maybe my interest in going places was never that great. But I do like planning journeys, a journey somewhere, sometime. I imagine going to Ravenna or the orient, and that's as far as it gets. The orient. Or Ravenna, Venice.

Whereas the lake exercises a great attraction: towards evening, when Gian is exhausted from all the work, when it doesn't seem to be getting anywhere, the lake remains a ray of hope. In an old fishing boat, the fisherman died of tuberculosis last year, Frau Gerster tells us, she tells us all about his suffering which we'd rather not hear about, all the details, in his boat, filled with his equipment, safety jackets, anchor, lights, distress flag and hook we move along the shore or across the lake, through the canal. We glide slowly among the branches of the old willow trees dipping into the water to the other side of the lake and follow the long strip of land which leads out to the island. Once there we head into the rushes and cut out the engine. In front of us, on the island, the trees tower up enormous and black against the light evening sky. Kites perch in the branches, looking for rabbits perhaps, with which the island is literally teeming; as you approach they dart away from you out of the open fields into the woods, they hop along the paths, the undergrowth is also teeming with them, they sit in their hundreds eating grass in the meadows.

We feel affected by what we view from the boat as immediately as if it were happening to us personally: the way the sky over the south-west end of the lake, over the last inlet becomes darker and darker, as if the light is turning slowly to slip away through a channel which begins at the horizon, as if the sun, already out of sight, is being sucked away ever more quickly through a duct of air while the wide curving sky above us, so dazzlingly multicoloured until a moment before, is transforming itself into a flat canvas whose colours become rapidly fainter and duller. The kites rise up from their posts and begin to circle above and the lake birds in the reeds all around us begin to call loudly.

'We had a carpenter in our street who had two Newfoundland dogs, he went down to the lake to groom them every day and he always took them to dog shows. Newfoundlands are animals which like people. They used to go out and fetch people in and when children in the lido swam out into the lake they used to call and the dogs would go out to them. They take them from behind if they can, get a hold and then swim with their bodies under the water, or they take them across their backs if they can, if someone's drowning it's just wonderful the way they do it. Sometimes we'd swim quite a long way out into the lake, then we'd yell and the dogs would come out to us, really fast. It's an instinct they've got, to fetch people in the water. But one of the Newfoundlands got killed by a train and the other one was as well, later on, by an express.

One time, it was winter, I heard shouts, they echoed across because of the wall. Oh, that must be children who've fallen in the water, I think as I run along the underpass, and there's one of them standing at the landing stage by the edge of the lake. Another one was down below clinging onto the ladder, so I grabbed his collar and hauled him out. The second one was holding on to the water pipe. I grabbed the first one and gave him a really good spanking. Then I got hold of the other one but he slipped away. I'm in for it with his mother now, I thought, because she'd always defended him so fiercely in the past, you weren't allowed to lay a finger on him, but this time she actually thanked me, although of course she did feel sorry for him: You know, his little botty was red for days.'

And so many people hit them, hadn't Frau Gerster said: 'Never hit a dog!'

'Yes, you've certainly got awareness, that's true, but not consciously, you just see what you see, it's not something you do on purpose. They were left to their own devices, the boys in the village and in the town, down by the lake. And you saw what they were up to and you told the parents they ought to be taking more notice of what their children, particularly their daughters were doing. You got different kinds of reactions. Sometimes it was: Mind your own business, and you knew you were getting nowhere. Then there were others who said: Thank you very much, but they're just more mature. There's a kind of impertinence there: It's none of anyone's business. There's not so much co-operation between adults and young people these days. Children knew it in the old days: if you caught one of them doing something then he realized it was time to stop, and he'd tell the others: I got a real dressing down from her. Oh yes, people knew how to behave then. He used to run away whenever he saw me. And now he's married and he always laughs when he sees me. It's because I always act spontaneously and the reaction comes later. It completely shatters me then, sometimes. That feeling.'

I know that feeling myself. I also often react too quickly and the *raison* doesn't come until later: I should have acted differently and I feel shattered. I've screamed at my battling children yet again, I nearly hit them. It was really the electrician I wanted to scream at.

It is illegal to install your own electrical wiring. The electricians come in without knocking and tramp all over the place, usually unexpectedly, never when you're prepared for them. If you try to render an acurate description of them you could say they were invented, exaggerated caricatures of figures from a novel. They seem self-assured, as if they were the ones in charge here, just tolerating our presence. They walk into the kitchen with its badly shutting doors just when I'm having a wash, go from the kitchen into the bedroom and back, shift some furniture and then, without any warning, they start drilling holes in the walls and ceiling without bothering to put anything away or cover anything up. One of them talks non-stop, it's impossible to work, to write, to read, even to think straight. I wish he was a character I'd invented, but then I hear him talking again. Sometimes the two of them perch themselves on a step or on the table, stare up in the general direction of some wiring in the ceiling and speculate upon it, half an hour at a time, the apprentice chattering on like a programmed talking automaton. They then continue to bore their channels into my newly cleaned and painted walls with renewed fervour.

They've got no time for our kind of conversion. I'll replace your oil, says the chatter-box who knocked a bottle of salad oil all over the floor and steps when he was drawing the wires through, so the old wooden boards are permanently stained. He doesn't bother to apologize because it's obvious to him that this flooring, like the stairs, will be covered over or replaced by something else, it can't possibly be left on show.

How would he go about renovating a house like this? Differently, he says. He'd rip everything out and replace what we've removed with new fittings, wall-cupboards, proper fitted kitchen, everything practical. And what did he mean by 'practical'? Standard units and tiles, for example, but then he'd never touch a building like this in the first place, there's no demand for this kind of property, it's only fit for the immigrant workers who don't know anything better and a few old people who've grown up in houses like this, inherited them and can't afford anything better. Young people do their conversions by buying two or three adjoining houses and knocking down the dividing walls, but that wasn't very practical because the floor levels in the houses are slightly different. And anyway, who wants all those stairs? People want to live on one floor these days, in villas outside the town, the electrician's apprentice tells me.

And then he disconnects the electricity, the light above the kitchen table goes out while I'm working on an illustration, a piece of work I'm supposed to be handing in tomorrow.

'Yes, you certainly learn a thing or two.' She, Frau Gerster, has done a lot in her time. 'In Biel I did twelve years at the same factory as my husband, I was at the bicycle factory for twelve years, that was until my son came along, checking parts, washing parts, after they'd been polished I washed them in petrol and chemicals. I could take it but there were others, I had assistants who couldn't. You can easily get rashes and that kind of thing from it. Just before I had my baby they got a sort of enormous washing machine which you put the parts into and there was a kind of conveyor belt inside it, but I had to do everything by hand, I had to inspect every part individually, sometimes there are cracks, scratches, and that's what I had to check for. I didn't use a magnifying glass, by the end I could tell just by looking, I could see things other people would never have noticed, about the colours, ours were white or grey, which ones were fired too hard and which ones weren't hard enough.'

All the different shades from dark blue through to grey, light grey, white as the steel cools and is then hardened by plunging it rapidly into water covered with a thick layer of oil, to chill it, I know all about that and I too could tell immediately from the colour which parts of a particular tool, an engraving instrument or a chisel, had hardened sufficiently, too little or too much, and which pieces were fired too hard. And according to the oxidization of a piece I can tell, could tell, if it was hot enough, if the metal would pour yet or if I would have to work at it more with the flame, turn it higher or lower, quickly, instantly, before the metal is scorched or starts to melt. Everything had to be done quick as lightning.

Or you can go, said the boss.

Work is work. If I'm enjoying what I'm working at, if I'm working conscientiously and well, I prefer to go slowly. Then you can go. And then? It's a 'drag', and certainly no fun if you have to file, solder and polish so many soldiers' identity bracelets every day.

'But I've never done piece-work, not I, I always refused, said: I'm sorry but I won't do pice-work, out of the question.

Because it's a 'drag'; the more you do, the more they expect from you, so I always said: Work is work. If I can see that it's good quality work, then I can work as fast as anyone, but if I see that it's poor work, I prefer to go slowly and inspect it more carefully. I wouldn't let myself be pressured, I told the foreman: I'm not doing piece-work, and I didn't keep a note of anything, nothing at all, so they had to pay me by the hour. I earned more money with my hourly pay than the people on piece-work. How did I manage it? The foreman trusted me. Of course, I was on our union committee for a long time. Right at the beginning, when the union started up in Biel, a few of us workers at the factory joined and we formed a committee and if the foreman wasn't happy about something you had to go and talk to him about it. I did a lot of work with them. I always got involved. Whenever anything went wrong I had to get involved, almost always. Sometimes when these fumes build up in the dipping rooms I've seen as many as five people faint because the manager put the wrong chemicals into the tanks and gases formed and rose up past the windows and I saw them all passing out, one after the other, there were windows all round the room but we couldn't get them open, so I broke them in, I took one of the bicycle parts and smashed them and then I carried the people out, one by one. They all watched me from outside, but no one came in to help, I got them out on my own. Only one of them had to be taken to the doctor. I always had to be there when anything happened. We had one worker who cut his fingers off in a press, four fingers. Of course, the word came: Frau Gerster, something's happened, and I went to the hospital with him at once.

Yes, you can change things, you can help, but you have to have a strong character to do it and you have to be able to give people good reasons, so they can see that you're right. And you also have to believe that you can do it, you have to be strong, it takes a lot of doing.'

The moment your mind is set on a goal it is encountered by many things. What is it? The moment I decide to help someone, to try to put something right or to change something, to change myself, or my surroundings or conditions which I and others don't like, what is it that I encounter when I've set myself this goal?

Sometimes it's just like something a pilot once told me: when you spot a tree, if you keep it in sight and are afraid you might fly into it, you've as good as crashed already.

When I think of the work in New York, of my inability to improve my working conditions, when I look at my room with the cracks in the walls and the wainscoting, when I look at my surroundings, when I see how, one after the other, the shutters along the street remain closed because the occupants have lost their jobs and moved out, when I hear the word 'fear' used increasingly in conversations, then I'm afraid that my wishes for myself and others are not going to be fulfilled in the way I would have liked. I should be working towards my goal, undaunted. But how?

'You have to be strong, have to have a strong character, it takes a lot of doing. Like with the trees, for example. I was over by the crane yesterday, I just dropped everything and went straight to the planners who are here because of the lake road, and I said: I want to know just where it's going, and I told them they were to show me the plans, and if it was going through here they weren't to lay a finger on those trees! Or I'll get a machine gun and the first person who so much as touches them is going to get it, and anyone else who's around!

But you'd be sent to prison!

And I said: They don't put sixty-five year old women in prison these days, they only get suspended sentences. So they lay out the map and showed it to me, and it said that they had to spare the trees, not one of them was to be touched, except for one branch at the front which was right against the road. So I told them: Fine. I'll let you have that branch, I mean, you'd have to be a bit abnormal not to let them have that one branch, but the others, you're not to touch those! I can guarantee that in the autumn when the leaves fall there won't be any leaves on that road. It's the wind from the lake that does it, I've watched it year in, year out. You have to give people good reasons.

Trust is very important. Just the way I look is very important. People respect you, they like you. I mean, there were times when you had to correspond with the union a lot, we had meetings and that kind of thing. I was always lucky when I went to the boss with a complaint, I never said anything in bad spirit, I always dealt with him in a friendly way, you just had to tell him exactly what the situation was. There are so many people on these committees who make the mistake of trying to force things through. All you do is inform people about the matter, tell them the facts and leave them until they realize you're right. You accomplish much more that way. And it's the same today, whether it's the government you're talking about or whatever, they keep trying to force things through and you can be pretty sure that the result won't be any good. It works if you've got patience, then you can talk to each other, discuss things, put forward some good ideas, give your honest opinion, that's what's most important. You've got two heads, and that makes two minds, and those two minds have to be able to work together. It's the same today, everywhere, it doesn't matter which country you're talking about, it's always the same, in any group of people there'll always be a few crafty ones who'll try to fool the others.'

The patience I display when I'm listening to Frau Gerster's detailed accounts is the kind of patience I'd need if I wanted to make myself understood, genuinely, thoroughly understood.

The way I myself passed out, collapsed because of the acid fumes, was ill for a while but couldn't talk to the boss, couldn't assert myself with him. He reduced my wages, never raised the minimum wage. And no trace of any solidarity.

Apart from the two other people in the workshop and the polisher I didn't know any workers in New York. A trade union? An old communist friend just shrugged his shoulders. But he did find me a better job where I was paid five dollars more.

You mustn't let yourself be pushed around! That's still the way of the world, and if I didn't learn to stand up for myself soon, I'd be condemned to this kind of life for ever, he told me.

But no, I don't want any part of this cat and mouse game, and I don't want to spend my time running up and down any imaginary ladders either, scrambling on, scrambling off: there must surely be a more intelligent, fairer way of living.

But no, he said, not yet unfortunately. And he ended up in the hands of the New York welfare authorities and died in a mental home.

My stories are already taking on that same tragic pattern, 'my' characters are suffering the same tragic fates as Frau Gerster's. I'm afraid now of returning to my own real siuation, to the various degrees of despondency, the feeling of the futility of it all. The lethargy alternating with hope: It's all right if you've got patience, trust, comfort from past achievements which can make carrying on worth while. The sporadic attempts to break free from all this, to escape from this cave of a house. Yet even these attempts are thwarted by my lassitude:

I stand in front of the class, look at the children's faces and feel too weak to fulfill eighteen sets of expectations, to hold out against these superior forces if they decide to pit themselves against me. My impatience prevents me from formulating my ideas, from communicating with the pupils, just as it prevents me from relating convincingly, talking about things I've thought through many times before so carefully:

Ask various people about their dogs and their relationships with their dogs. Talk to them about their dogs and then about themselves, try to get through to these people via their dogs, try to get to know them. Try to get them to give a picture of themselves by talking about their dogs, I tell the pupils. Just as I wasn't haunted by the fear: that's not the way to do it, you'll never get through to children like that, the feeling of talking away at them with a sack over my head.

'It's all right if you've got patience.'

'You could tell him to do anything you liked,' says Frau Gerster, 'absolutely anything. Mongrels are more intelligent than other dogs, in my opinion anyway, but perhaps other kinds of dogs can be intelligent too.

He had four different breeds in him: his mother was a mongrel, Pomeranian mixed with Senne Hound, but a little one. And his father had poodle and some dachshund in him. He had something of all of them: from head to neck, down to his front paws his hair was Bernese Senne Hound, quite smooth. He didn't have to be clipped, quite smooth, lovely smooth short hair. And his body was Pomeranian, his body was that lovely Pomeranian shape, and his muzzle, his nose and front paws were poodle. But his ears were Bernese Senne Hound again, they hung down. If he wanted to walk along very proudly he'd let his ears waggle, he was a perfect scream! I groomed him very regularly, because of the long hair underneath, that's why his coat was always so shiny, and the beet for his blood, his blood was always pure, that's why he was so lively.

Taking them out every day is a real must, but I just don't feel like it any more, which is a shame because otherwise I'd have noticed, I wouldn't have been taken in like I was.

The way they managed it with the other road, the one which goes out to the cemetery and which had trees all along it, was by starting work on it at six o'clock one morning, it was because of the road, they said they were going to widen it and the pavement, but the road is just the same now as it always was and the pavement, the only change is that the trees have gone! We collected signatures from the whole street and put them on the table in the town hall, but no one took any notice of them, they just ordered the soldiers, we had soldiers round then, to fell the trees. That's how it happened. Then I thought: wait a minute. I didn't say anything I just took all the signatures and everything to Bern. As soon as they said that the trees down by the lake were to be chopped down I had photos taken, someone from the newspaper did it for me, I spoke to the editor and he said: that'll go into the paper, just as it is, and down at the harbour I had a big sign made: HELP US SAVE OUR TREES and over four Sunday afternoons I got more than 3,000 signatures, no foreigners, all Swiss, and I had carbon copies of them all so they couldn't deny the signatures existed, so I actually had proof. I got official backing from the Society for the Improvement of Local Amenities, the Nature Preservation Society, the Society for the Protection of the Lakeside, the Forestry Commission, about eight organizations all in all. And I went to Bern with all this, I didn't give it to the local authorities here, they would just have ignored it, like they did before.'

Each to his own, says the man who's installing the central heating, grinning as he watches Gian and Patrick, drenched in sweat even though they're down to their swimming trunks, perched on long ladders up in the roof struggling with the silvery, prickly glass-fibre insulating material. This is how we like it.

And we like the way things are here, in spite of a few minor difficulties in getting used to it. On the whole our average income is pretty much the same as those of our neighbours, frequently it's lower. Our life style here is determined more by financial considerations than by aesthetic ones.

I cannot see anything beautiful in an enormous, ostentatious switch panel, the electrician's pride and joy, which he has installed in the stairway to catch the eye. (And what's it going to cost?) Without its cover, with its countless multicoloured wires still visible, I would have liked it, would even have considered it something worth displaying. No, no way, the electrician defends himself, that would be unfinished and, therefore, ugly; he only finds it pleasing when it's quite finished, you always get the conflict of opinion between the professional and the layman, he tells me. And it's against fire-regulations to hide it behind a curtain.

'Yes, I've done a thing or two in my time. When the children were small it was a case of having to look after them as best you could, until they started work. And when my husband died they had to give me a pension, he'd paid all the contributions for a wife's pension should she be widowed, so they had to pay me my share, and there was supposed to be a widow's pension as well, but I saw little enough of that, I could never have managed on it, that's why I kept the boats on and just kept working until I couldn't manage it any longer. And I sold them for a good price, considering all the unemployment these days. All that unemployment, but they still ride round on *Töff*, all the same, a *Töff* is a motorbike, even the ones who haven't got money for anything else. The running costs for a boat are just too high, you have to overhaul them every spring, there's always something needs doing and if the profit you've made by the autumn is so small that you can hardly cover the following spring's expenses, you have nothing left to show for all your work, then there's no point in doing it any more. So I took advantage of the opportunity when I was ill, it was a good reason for selling. And I'm really pleased, now the widow's pension is bigger, it doesn't appeal to me in the slightest any more, I haven't got any of that old drive left telling me "you've got to make it".'

With her *benefiz*, with the money she'd got saved, she had her stairway done up. Full of pride, Frau Gerster shows me her practical 'Succoflor' floors, the 'Pavatex' panelling and her fine new curtains.

The views, the taste of the experts: gadgets, prefabricated tiled walls, prefabricated plaster walls, prefabricated fitted kitchens, fitted cupboards, prefabricated mirrored bathroom cabinets, prefabricated windows and doors, quite good some of them, some of them very good, good and expensive. *Renovating your flat? Put your trust in us, we'll guarantee you satisfaction.* And the homeliness you can buy from the expert next door, in the shop window: the frilly lace curtains, the brocade curtains, lampshades with ruffles, pseudo-gothic mirror frames and cloths edged with gold lace on antique, pseudo-antique polished furniture. French interiors à la Vuillard, not the genuine thing unfortunately, but what could be nicer than a reproduction!

I wonder if here, among the craftsmen and workers the demand determines the supply or the supply the demand to a greater extent than usual. The electrician never stops to question his demands, neither does Frau Gerster, they don't ask themselves whether what they are offered is really what they want or whether they have just learnt to want what is offered them, offered them as something which is the mark of someone else, a civil servant, a company director, etc., someone who is better off than they are. It's banal, we've known that for a long time, and yet it carries on as if no one had realized, and that, too, we realize. Frau Gerster was well satisfied with the service she was given.

'Young Karl used to help me with hiring out and cleaning the boats since I also always used to give a hand with the cleaning. He was good because he could speak three languages. He spoke Italian, French and German and I could trust him, he was very reliable. You told him what you wanted and he did it, I could send him back up to the house ten times a day to fetch things, go and get this, go and get that; he was free to go in and out as he pleased, he always said yes: This is like a second home to me, I like it here. And he'd come back with everything, I'd tell him where it was and he'd find it, and that's why we trusted him. Nothing ever went missing, no money or anything. He filched some change once from my desk, but it was foreign money which I always put in a cup. And he only did it so he could go to France with the school, it was an exchange and his mother said: You can go, but I'm not giving you more than so much. And then the boy found out that there was money here and took it. I knew about the French trip, of course, and I said to him: all right Karl, let's put some money on one side, tips and that sort of thing and that'll be enough, but it wasn't. He thought he wouldn't be able to go so he just took the money and changed it at the bank. Later, I wanted to pay for something and found there was nothing in it, I suspected him immediately because no one else had been there.

So I said: I have to go to the shops and then to the bank. Are you coming? He didn't suspect it was because of him. I'd been to the bank first and asked if they would recognize him, and as I walked into the bank the cashier says: Yes, that's him.

Please don't tell my parents, he begged, or I won't be able to go.

So I say: all right, I'm a reasonable person. I've always been able to trust him up to now. I'll turn a blind eye and won't say anything. The parents must have noticed something because he had the money, but they didn't say anything. And afterwards my trust in him gradually came back, we kept everything locked up and I slowly came to trust him with more and more again, going up to the house and fetching things for me. And it never happened again. I had him for five years.

I simply can't be bothered any more, the operation really took it out of me, and while I'm not one hundred per cent fit I'm just not interested, but I do need to be with people now and again, a little, that's what I miss. That's when I drop everything and I go down to the lake, I just have to. I don't regret selling everything, the boats and the *pedalos*, not at all, that proves I'm still not one hundred per cent fit yet. The doctor told me it takes time. It's nothing dangerous, nothing cancerous, we've made sure of that, it's rare for a fat person to get anything cancerous.

When I came out of hospital I was sent up to Leysin to convalesce. My sister came to visit me almost every Sunday and one day, the Sunday before I was coming home, she says:

Have I got a blow for you!

What's wrong?

The Jarjems are leaving.

But don't they have to give notice? say I. This has been on the books since the spring, she says, at Madame Serova's funeral old Jarjem asked the priest if there was room for them in any of the old people's homes.

Well, they ought at least to wait until I get home, I've always kept an eye on them, I did everything I could for them!'

La vieille dame soviétique, is what the electrician from next door calls the old Russian lady, but wrongly. 'Soviet', she understood the word, the name must have sounded like a term of derision to her. But she couldn't communicate, couldn't explain anything, clear up any misunderstandings. All they know here is that people fled from their country, *tant pis*.

The flight, that reluctant departure. The experience of being handed over to someone, of having no control over your own destiny, of simply having to wait. It means you're being deported, being forced to do something you don't want to do, having to endure something you don't want to happen. From one place to the next. Places you'd never have chosen yourself, Hong Kong, for example. Only to be sent on, God knows when, to the next place, to another camp and maybe, eventually, God knows when, to be one of the ten or twelve lucky ones to be given refuge in Switzerland. A refugee home, later, your own home, a normal life when you're old and ill and when it's far too late for that kind of life.

'They didn't want for anything but they felt they were being ignored. There are some places which accept refugees, which would never let any harm come to these people, and then there are other places which put pressure on them, that is they stifle them, and those are places where the people don't know what it's like to be poor, where they live a life of plenty, they can't possibly imagine what it means to be poor, there's a kind of hatred there in places like that, while it's just the opposite in those other places, people are friendlier to them, motherly, people take them in like you would a child from a foreign place. It's all right to take in a foreign child if you know you can replace its mother, but not otherwise. I'm quite against that. There are many people who take children in when they're little, if they're cute, and then when they've reached a certain age they start resenting them, that hurts the child and the children sometimes turn out to be no good.

So these refugees didn't establish such close links with people here, they felt they'd been pushed to one side and they suffered a lot among themselves, they didn't write to each other much, hardly at all. But they had everything they needed, they had some money in the first place and then they got some from the refugee home and a lot came from America and all in all they had more than our people had. The orthodox Russians help each other out.

But at the hospital the first thing the nurse asked me was: where's the jewellery? That was fatal, I panicked. We didn't find anything, nothing at all, that's all Madame Serova had: earrings, her watch, then she had rings, she wore rings on every finger, all gold, and in the hospital they put them in a little bag. The Serov's are buried here, both of them, and they've got lovely gravestones, really wonderful, the orthodox Russians have a different kind of cross from us, one with a diagonal line through it, their gravestones cost over 2,000 francs, she'd put money to one side for that and given it to Madame Jarjem.

Anyway, the Jarjems did delay their departure, but the moment I was back they thought it would be all right to go. So

I said to them: you've known about this for long enough, you could easily have told me you were thinking of moving out in the autumn. But no, they packed everything up and left. They were allowed to take their furniture with them but they left everything else so I then had to do the clearing up, all the junk they left behind, the moment I got back from Leysin. The room had to be completely redecorated afterwards, he had blocked up all the cracks the moment they felt any draught, at the slightest draught he would plug up the cracks and the more cracks he blocked up the more our wood panelling deteriorated.'

The cracks in the ceiling from which all the dust trickles whenever you take a step upstairs, dust which has accumulated between the floorboards over the decades, which might go back a hundred years.

The broad cracks in the walls, which you only don't see because of the wallpaper, the wallpaper which is torn, which has been painted over in many places.

In the front room, the children's room, one of our predecessors has roughly plastered over the cracks in the wall, thick bulging patches run diagonally across the wall underneath the green wallpaper. On each of these patches I paint a palm tree trunk, seven palm trees, the children paint in the branches and leaves, birds and mountains and water, a castle, a bear and sailing boats on the walls.

There's no point in plastering over the cracks in the walls, no point in patching them up, says Frau Gerster, for the foundations of these buildings rise and fall just as the level of the water in the lake rises and falls, depending on the time of year.

'You can patch the cracks as much as you like but they'll always open again. It's just like the wood panelling, when you heat the house, the more you plug the cracks the more our wood panelling cracked. We had cracks of up to six centimetres because of the heating and there being no air, the flat had been completely renovated three years before and afterwards we had to have the panelling done again, but differently this time. That's what happens when you're too kind hearted. We liked them, we really had nothing against them, nothing at all, and if she needed anything, or he did, then they'd come up and see me and if they had to go to the local authorities for anything, then I used to go for them, he was over eighty, he wasn't allowed to get too excited or he'd get trouble with his heart, so it was always me who went.

You felt sorry for them, I mean, the way I thought was: you have to help the refugees, it's not their fault, and you have to stop to think what it would be like if we had to leave our homes like that, had to leave everything behind, you have to remember that they probably suffer a lot spiritually as well, you know about that yourself, perhaps.

You can feel sorry for them but at the same time there has to be a limit somewhere; you also have to remember that we used to have a lot of poor people of our own, although there certainly aren't many left today. There are still poor people in the remote valleys here, but many of them simply won't let themselves be helped, it's a kind of false pride, it makes them feel that their conscience, their character is being threatened, they want the pride of knowing they can control their own destiny, and that's a false pride.

Foreigners are people, just like anyone else, there are poor ones and there are rich ones, and then there are cocksure ones, you throw them out, the ones who don't behave properly.

Of course, every case is different, you have to find out why he's being cocky, or why he's been saying crazy things, or if he's been stirring up feelings among other people, it's such a complicated business. For example, there was one of them on the television last night and he had a real way with words but there was never any mention of the fact that he was an absolute good-for-nothing, no one said anything about that, they didn't ask where he came from or what he did, they just showed you that foreigners are being sent out of the country, not that he wasn't behaving normally.'

But there are others who are being sent out of the country who are 'behaving' quite correctly. It's quieter in our street now, some of the seasonal workers didn't return in the spring. But there's still something of a bond between the people who live here. It's disquieting to realize that this bond, the unity of the structure of this street, stems from the dilapidated state of the housing and is fed by exploitation. A house instead of copper shares: a transaction, then forget, wait. That people are allowed to let accommodation in that kind of state, even if the tenants, mostly foreigners, have never known anything better. That this kind of thing happens, even when it's not allowed, and no one gets punished for it!

In the floors of the toilets in this building, TUALETEN was written on one door, holes had been knocked, as if with an axe, so that the water which flowed from the leaky pipes, could drain away: into the ceiling of the loo below. She has made numerous complaints, explains Mademoiselle Alice, but nothing has ever been done. And when we took the house, the owner advised us to move into Mademoiselle Alice's flat as it was the only one which was anywhere near fit for occupation. The old spinster had had a boiler put in and painted everything without asking the owner, so we were not under any obligation to reimburse her, the owner said.

'Him on the television, the foreigner, we had him here for a while, I threw him out after two months, he was so vulgar, so dirty! So I said to my sister: he hasn't got any contract with us yet, I'm not keeping him! It's all very well for him to turn sanctimonious on television! I was all set to ring up and get them to ask him how he thought he'd been behaving, how he'd been carrying on, they should ask a few questions round here in Seewyler, they'd get a different answer here, they were thrown out of the place they moved to after a month and a half, they borrowed 10,000 francs, got all new furniture, so much that they could hardly get it all in the flat, put on all kinds of airs and graces, a fantastic coat and a television, a colour one, and they were expensive four years ago, but they didn't pay a thing, not even to their new landlord. And someone like that gets on television!'

Mademoiselle Alice puts lettuces on our doorstep or she brings a basket of cherries, later tomatoes, courgettes, whatever happens to be ripe in her brother's garden. Or she comes with a bowl of ratatouille, she's made too much.

How's the house going? asks the butcher's wife: aren't you getting fed up with it? She tells me they've been renovating their old house on the main road for eight years now and every year they get more allergic to the noise of the traffic. We're still hoping we'll get used to the noise eventually.

I look at the clock: five to eleven. As I do so, cooking smells reach my nose, fried onions: I don't have to look at the clock at this time any more, I know it smells the same every day at this time. Soon I'll be able to tell who cooks what, just as I've been able to distinguish the different voices for a long time now, which one belongs to whom, the raucous, very loud voice of the old Spanish lady. And I'm pleased I can't speak Spanish, that I only have to hear and don't have to understand what's being said.

Have you still got your rabbit? the Spanish lady shouts out to me in French the moment she spies me up in the attic. I take the animal from its cage and hold it out. She holds up her little granddaughter just like I'm holding the rabbit, turns the little one's head in my direction and she laughs and waves at me, or the animal. When we meet each other out on the street the Spanish lady always asks: Is the front door open? And I later find a big bunch of cabbage leaves on the step.

'And then you get someone like us on television, a decent,

respectable kind of person, never had any trouble with anyone and no one's got anything against him, but he can't stand up for himself, whereas someone who's got so much to hide has to play it big like that. Foreigners are people just like everyone else, we used to be foreigners even though father had never been to Italy, only during the 1871 war, that's where he was born. Father's father was a rag-picker in France and when his mother got in the family way he told her she should go to Italy, anything could happen with a war on. A rag-picker is someone who collects old material and junk, a rag and bone man, he went all through France on foot and had a *roulotte*, the sort they use in the Jura now for excursions and weekends, or for holidays, but my grandfather slept in his and went all over the place collecting scrap, and that's how he got through the '71 war. There were various depots for the scrap, factories for material and the like, he took the scrap there, got money to buy kitchen ware and then sold the china, glazed kitchen ware, white cups, I've still got one of them here, and he had shoes and socks as well. And he also had a horse for the *roulotte*, this caravan, the sort they used to have. We always used to sleep in it in the holidays, that was quite something, that was a real holiday for us, when we were allowed to go and visit grandfather in his *roulotte*.'

My father's father with whom I used to spend my holidays almost every year, usually during the hunting season. My memories of this grandfather are still very clear, this grandfather who could spit from one corner of the verandah, where the dining table was, to the other, into a spittoon or a glass. My sister and I would sit in front of our mugs, mugs of warm milk which we didn't like. And the longer we put off drinking the milk the thicker the skin on the milk became. My grandfather used to love eating the skin of the milk, and having to watch, or even think of him just about to spit or fish the skin out of the milk was enough to make you puke.

You shouldn't say that!

I know, but you shouldn't do that sort of thing either.
Why not?

Apart from the spitting, this grandfather was a delightful, energetic person who used to tell me a lot about his childhood. Was he the youngest of nine or was it twelve? I can't remember, but I do remember that my great-grandfather was a smallholder and a linen bleacher; I see mountainsides all covered with white cloth. And I see my grandfather wandering between Silesia and Switzerland as a travelling weaver, and from Switzerland to Moravia. He lived through three wars, but he was never a soldier because he was too young for the 1871 war and too old for the First and Second World Wars. He probably told me so many stories because he liked me; it's because of him, not my parents, that I'm called Erica, his favourite name, he loved heather, unlike me. It's too dry and unassuming for me. He wasn't unassuming, he was energetic and often so loud that he frightened us. That's why, at breakfast, on the verandah we watched the skin slowly forming on the milk, silently suppressing our disgust.

This grandfather used to go out hunting and sometimes he would take me with him. I had to fasten leather gaiters round my calves, these hard leather gaiters came in all different sizes, even for little children, to protect you against the vipers we were always warned about whenever we went to pick berries or wandered a few yards from the house. But at night, when the paraffin lamps or candles could only cast little pools of light in the rooms and everything lay cloaked in darkness, when there was nothing and no one to protect me, the vipers would appear and wind their way up the bedposts, black and silent and quick. It was only during the daytime that I was protected against them, up to the knees, when we tried to fight our way through the jungle of raspberry and blackberry canes, when we slipped across forest clearings, over the meadows and through the high forests.

So I knew all about hunting even before a hunter married me. You have to let a hunter be a hunter, for he can never change.

Ever since I was a tiny child I've heard hunting stories, stories about a particular chamois, or doe or stag, each with it's own, special name; about particular 'deer trails' and sites known only to the intitiated, to which the story-teller would lead you to, every turn, every tree, every stone, a description accurate to the last detail. The same stories from an uncle and from my father, stories from one hunter, two, three, so that when I fell in love with a hunter or when he fell in love with me I was not, unlike his previous girlfriends, scared off by his hunting stories, not even when the number of hunters was swelled to four by the father-in-law, brother-in-law and family doctor. And soon I shall be celebrating the silver anniversary of my marriage to a hunter in spite of the stag, chamois, doe, fox, brown hare, and white hare, badger, marmot, squirrel, weasel, marten, wood grouse, black cock, rock partridge, snow grouse, wild duck, pheasant, grey partridge and quail hunts and all the other hunting stories.

This energetic, hunting grandfather was married to my gentle Swiss grandmother. The wife of my other grandfather, my extraordinarily peace-loving grandfather, had no choice other than to be energetic and she anticipated often the worst. As I had a completely different relationship with each of my grandparents and still do have, even though they've been dead a long time now, as I can identify traits of all four of them in me, some more pronounced, others less so, as I fear some of them and encourage others, I've written little so far about the peace-loving grandfather and the gentle grandmother, because what I need most at the moment is the energy which my father's father and my mother's mother had.

'So my grandmother went to Italy and my father was born there so he was an Italian, his sisters were born in France and they're French. That's why we were born Italians. When he wanted to get married he had to go all the way to Italy to get the papers, that's the only time he was ever in Italy. I don't know if my grandfather ever got naturalized, but he died in France. My grandmother too, but we never knew her.

My grandfather had a little shack where he could keep his horse, and he had one or two pigs as well, because he sometimes earned quite good money, and a few chickens and they all slept together, all in the same room. He died in 1918. He had kept the horse in there all winter, it was a hard winter, and in the spring, he had a big meadow as well, he let the horse out and stupidly he wound the loop of the reins round his arm to hold the horse, and the horse went wild and pulled him along, the horse quite lost its head and dragged him along the ground after it for several miles, across the fields and the stones and everything. His insides were completely shattered. He lived for three days. Then someone found him, the horse was standing next to him, it had calmed down by then. They took him home and contacted us and we went there to him. Yes, my grandfather was a rag-picker, but that's not a gipsy, oh no.

But my mother, she was descended from Napoleon, her mother was a Butzberg, a *von* Butzberg, and there was a special stamp on all her papers, a mark. When I went to see the palace in Brussels with my daughter, that's right I went to Brussels with my daughter, it was just at the time when they were celebrating Leopold's centenary, Leopold the First, or the Second, and they open both the palaces to the public, the private palace and the other one. The crowds! Just when we happened to be in Brussels. Anyway, I said to Dorli: Look, we were in the Napoleon Room, we can see where they slept at last, *les ancêtres* of our old relations. An aunt, one of my mother's aunts, died in Olten and they told us there that she was descended from Napoleon, so we immediately checked this up. Which is why I said to Dorli: *Tu vois, notre parenté,* our family still has its royal bed there, look! And there was an attendant standing near us in the room who heard this and disappeared. Then he reappeared with King Baudouin! Heading straight towards me. We went on to look at his

Philadelphia stamp collection, he's got the most wonderful stamp collections in the world, has Baudouin, has the King. Then he says to us: *On voit bien qu'il y a de la décence, parce que vous vous intéressez pour les timbres.* So I say to him: *C'est interessant, ça.* Then he gave me his hand and said:

C'est vous alors, les parentées de Napoleon?

J'ai dit: Oui, soit disant, car les papiers de ma maman, mais moi, je n'ai jamais appuyé là-dessus, je ne le savais pas, and I explained it all to him. Then we were invited into the palace, both of us, and I told Dorli: Make sure you behave properly, all right, whatever happens, all right, just remember these people know how to behave! I never get worried by that kind of thing when I'm with people who matter. Anyway, he showed us all over the castle then, where they have the assemblies, local ones, the city ones and the national ones and the royal assemblies as well, we were allowed to see everything, even Leopold I's little railway. He has a little railway built in the palace courtyard under the arcades, it's a big thing, a lovely heirloom, with the tracks under the arcades in the palace courtyard, and they also had an exhibition by Rubens, the painter, in one of these buildings, and there was one painting of four negroes, gaiety, *désespoir, éternité* and something else, four negro heads and he gave the first reprint of it to Dorli. We saw whole rows of them, they'd had them brought from America specially, that really was an exhibition, the ultimate, it was lovely! You simply couldn't tear yourself away. And he stayed with us, Baudouin did, he enjoyed it as much as we did, we had a real good laugh together and I thought to myself: it doesn't make any difference, him being a king. He wrote to me a few times after that, I've still got them, the letters, they're locked away.'

Her father was Italian, not a gipsy, oh no. At the time of my birth my father was a Czech, although born in Moravia; he was Austrian like all other Czechs until the end of the First

World War, until the founding of the CRS, the First Czech Republic. So I was Czech for the first eight years of my life, until the *Anschluss*. Then, because we spoke German like almost everyone in the area, we became Germans, without anyone consulting us about it. At the end of the Second World War, when the CSSR was founded, we became stateless. Later, Austrians. Then, after ten years in the USA, my father, my mother and my brother and sisters became Americans. In the meantime I had become a Swiss citizen because I had returned to Switzerland after two years in New York and married here. All of us, out of necessity, rarely of our own free-will, had fought or trailed our way through alternating periods of war and peace and many different countries, but we're not gipsies. Oh no, I have lived continuously for twenty-two years in the same village and have only moved house once.

'Yes, yes, and the King of Liechtenstein, have I shown you the crown with the big pearl on it which he sent me? The Prince of Liechtenstein. I took him in my boat a few times. I always get gooseflesh when I pick it up, it's gold, how lovely it is! As a souvenir of the Queen of the Lake. I don't wear it, I'm afraid of losing it, I've got it locked away. My daughter or my son will get it one day, under a picture, they can hang it under a photo — how lovely it is!'

The Liechtenstein Castle up above my grandfather's garden. I could tell Frau Gerster all about that castle, about the gothic chapel and the collection of paintings and about one of the princes who all of a sudden was no longer a prince because his family forbade him to use his title or his name.
   The idea that my family could take my name away from me because of some impropriety, could forbid me to use the name that's mine just because I do something that isn't usually done, because I'm caught smuggling or, what's even worse if

seldom punishable, writing something I shouldn't write.

Anyway, the Liechtensteins had several estates and castles. True, I'm not interested in castles and princes, but one of them was, still is, in Sternberg in Moravia and towers up above the garden which used to belong to my peaceloving grandfather. The garden, which was said to have been the castle park earlier, was filled by my grandfather with countless different varieties of flowers, many of them quite rare, and a few vegetables for my grandmother's sake, but even those were the more unusual kinds which weren't so well-known in those days. And when he stayed at the castle he, the one who at that time was still a prince, must have had an extraordinary view from the south-west facing windows, out over an enormous brightly flowering chaos, all through spring, summer and autumn, because the garden was very large. Now it's all gone to seed.

Today, the public can go and look round this former private castle which is now a People's Property. It's open every day and one coach after another winds its way up there, five hundred to a thousand visitors every day; feudal splendour interests the citizens of communist countries. An interest I would have expected more among conservatives, but Frau Gerster, former members of the workers' committee, tells me differently.

'He was walking by, the prince was, when he saw the sign *Boats for hire* and he wanted to bring the little ones, the three children, and he came a few more times after that. It was in the paper here several times, in a tribute to me, who was called the Princess of the Lake. That I'd known how to add a touch of humour to the trips as well: *she was also a clever, knowledgeable woman who was well-informed about everything.*

I was never able to take him with me on the boat, he howled all the way from here to the island, all round the island and from the island back here again, from sheer joy! Then he rushed up to me and then up to the passengers and he barked and came back to me, because I sometimes used to tell the people something about the area, about Seewyler, all kinds of things, and he barked because he wanted to tell a story as well, but that wasn't very nice for the passengers. I just went round the island, I had to do it quickly, had to make sure I could get back as quickly as possible. I could never know whether anything had happened or not. Yes, there were the *pedalos*, and there was mother as well.'

The middle of the lake, a burning white sheet which approaches me from the bay at the other end of the lake, getting wider and bigger, reminds me of the burning magnesium my grandfather once showed me in his garden. The flaming white sparks of magnesium, I've never seen anything so blinding, brighter than if you were to look right into the sun, in front of a dark barn wall, and nearby the flowerbeds with the tomato plants covered in shiny red tomatoes, small as cherries. I find the same variety thirty years later in a seed catalogue. I haven't seen burning magnesium since then, but there's the same phosphorescence on the lake today.

'So when mother became ill I only used to go out with the boat when there were enough people asking, when there were six, seven, eight people with me, never if there were only one or two there, because of mother. I used to have to go up to her a lot. In the end I had a girl looking after her. She wasn't there half the time, but I knew the dog would guard her for me. He could sense that I was entrusting him with a great responsibility, that I was putting great trust in him. It's an instinct we don't have, which the higher animals don't have, this instinct, they can sense things that are going to happen and if you really watch them you can sometimes prevent things happening, you can learn from them. And the day she died we didn't bring him into the bedroom when she died, he didn't come into the room again, just so he understood: it's all over, she's

not going to be there any more. We were all there round her,
he just sniffed around and went off. Tail between his legs, he
went downstairs and then up to the second floor, the third
floor, and didn't come down again. And even when the
visitors were there, for the funeral, he didn't show himself, he
lay in his box and didn't make a sound. And when the funeral
was over he cheered up again. That's interesting. To start
with he'd go into her room, two or three steps, then he'd
remember she wasn't there any more and he'd come back.
Yes, we had fun sometimes and mother had fun with him.
The way he used to guard mother; I was able to leave her in
bed and go and see to the boats. As I was saying, he was
overintelligent, really. If there was no one with her he would
open the door and dash to the lake to get me, he'd race around
and bark and bark so I knew I had to go to her. And as I say,
this was without any training, nothing. They knew what it
meant, down at the lake, all the women, when they saw him
dashing round the corner to get me, sometimes he'd almost
overshoot it. Or when she had to go to the toilet, she couldn't
make it downstairs, couldn't get out of bed any more, so she'd
say to him: Get mummy! And off he'd dash. I wasn't at all
concerned about her, far less concerned than if I'd had a
person with her, because the dog had this instinct, a really
sharp instinct for everything, and that's rare.'

My grandmother's last illness; I can see her lying in a light
hospital room in front of a big open window, fruit trees
outside the window, a mountainous country which she
certainly got used to over the fifteen years she was there, but
which was never really home. My Viennese grandmother
never really came to terms with 'Swiss German'.

I can't see her climbing the steps of this house. Mountains
of mending pile up in the laundry room, enormous holes in
socks and pullover sleeves which would not have pleased her.
My husband lets an unruly mane of hair grow, sometimes a
beard, a beard he used to have cut off occasionally for her

sake. My younger children behave in a way which would never have been possible if she had been around, they are missing out on the upbringing which not only her own children but also her grandchildren, myself and my own three eldest children received. Many of 'her' words, like *Jause*, *Spagat*, *Krampus*, *Altan*, *Kredenz* and *Kasserole* are completely foreign to my children. My grandmother would never have managed these stairs with her stiff knee and would probably have seen us living like this as a real come-down. I would also have found it difficult to tell her about the arrival of a fifth child. For before she could register pleasure in anything, she always had to go through every imaginable misfortune, every conceivable affliction which might result; a child could easily be deaf, dumb, simple, incurably ill. She had considered our fourth child to be an irresponsible temptation of providence, which up to now had been so unexpectedly abundant.

She herself had often fared badly at the hands of fate. But as she always anticipated the worst, when it actually arrived she bore it with admirable composure. Whereas I, after hearing her talk about dying for thirty years, could hardly grasp the fact that she, at the age of eighty-six, actually was on the verge of death. And with the death of that grandmother, who was the real hub of the family, a whole world which had survived with her, finally disappeared.

Rather than these hospital visits, I prefer to think of my grandfather in the garden in Sternberg, bending over a flower bed or the cold frames, or crouching among his shrubs. It was a garden which could be mine one day, he said, because I was the only one in the family to show a genuine interest in his plants, to take a real pleasure in his gardening, an activity which my grandmother, with growing concern, regarded merely as a hobby. My grandfather tried to allay her concern and refute her accusations with astonishing calculations about how he could earn so many crowns or marks for every Maréchal Niel rose, how every plant in the greenhouse could produce so many buds, so many roses multiplied by the number of rose bushes in the two green houses would yield a sum which would cover all the money he put into them in no time, and then there were the strawberries, the nursery plants, the seedlings etc.

Yes, but you give everything away!

It's beautiful here already in the Volksgarten, the Rathaus-park and the Votivpark, he wrote, my grandfather wrote from Vienna, shortly before his death, in a letter to his son in Paris (the son who had served in the Czech Legion during the war but who, after the war, had been refused citizenship of the CSSR, had not even been allowed to return to the country because his mother tongue was German), beds of tulips, pansies, and marguerites were already in flower, he wrote. And the magnificent Japanese cherries, magnolias and almond and apricot trees.

After their expulsion from Czechoslovakia he and my grandmother and one of their daughters ended up in a flat in the heart of Vienna belonging to a great-aunt, a flat which had been built to accommodate half that number of people. After much long and tortuous journeying.

He could walk for hours every day in these gardens, he wrote, in fact it was pleasanter here and he had far less work than in Sternberg, and he was no longer at all concerned about the old place, since all his friends there had either gone away or were dead. (A sentence I cry over, but secretly, for in my family it's not the done thing to display sorrow, to admit to feeling sorrow about something which has gone for ever, let alone to write about it.) And all the millions and millions of plants, all the tulips, and narcissi thrived here just as they did back home, wrote my grandfather, all the plants which for fifty years had slowly been revealing the secrets of existence to him.

I haven't got that far yet. I'm still too full of indignation. Only occasionally, when I'm pregnant or immediately after giving birth, when I'm with little children, or, occasionally, with older ones, sometimes when I catch sight of a person, or hear a tune, or see some flowers, the 'secrets of existence', are revealed to me too, for a moment.

But together with my indignation, in spite of my reluctance simply to accept outrages without protest, as the way of the world, I seem to have the gift, like this grandfather, for making the best of circumstances, wherever I happen to be, for recognizing the good side of every situation: the Czech farmer's family, the seven shoemakers, the wonderful years in Zurich and my lovely aunt there, the basement in New York, Idella and Toni who disappeared without trace, the country around Mamaroneck, the Long Island Sound, all that was, and still is, lovely and good, the Engadine as well, and the lake here — and this house is going to be ready one day too.

Gian is at work again already, with mortar and plaster he has made good the damaged patches of wall, but how can he possibly repair or replace everything else, the cables which are hanging down everywhere, the rotten panelling? He's perched on a ladder, so busy that he can't or won't give me an answer: the only way ever to finish all this is probably not to think about it, just to apply yourself to one job at a time. Sometimes Gian's way of working up to fourteen hours a day without a break worries me, worries me more and more every time he does it. 'You don't stop to consider your own health, that you might ruin it with all the work, you don't think, you just go on working. And in the end you've worn away all your body's resistance, your nerves are strained, your morale is rock bottom.'

'Anyway, so the lake is very dangerous. There was a man once, he'd come from a hospital, a mental hospital, he tried to commit suicide. And someone, a gentleman, a bank manager came running along, shouting: Frau Gerster, come and look, what is it? And he looked like a balloon. That was his overall, the air trapped in the back of his overall, in fact it kept him afloat when what he was trying to do was drown himself, down by the steam boat jetty it was, there are steps there, two steps and that's where he went into the water. So we took the boat hooks and tried to reach him, and when we got hold of him, he grabbed the pole and tried to fight us off, so we were able to draw him to the edge. He hadn't swallowed much water but we put him on his stomach and thumped him on the back a few times, just in case. Then we took him along to the police station. We didn't tell him we were taking him there, but that's where we took him, just as he was, in his wet clothes, we told him we were going to the welfare people. He didn't want to say where he came from, all he said was — what was it? It's my wife's fault, it's my wife's fault, he kept saying over and over again. But he was disturbed, he had come from the mental hospital, after all. Anyway, I told the policeman he ought to get hold of the man's wife, and he, the policeman, shouldn't wear his uniform, otherwise he'd be frightened. So we made him coffee, then the policeman came in plain clothes, and they questioned him and he told them where he came from. And then they took him back there. He had run away and tried to commit suicide, he'd tried it two or three times already but they'd caught him. The bank manager had seen him but didn't realize what it was. But I saw at once that it was a body, you know, with the legs and the head down in the water, which makes a balloon if you are wearing an overall. He could still have touched the bottom there, it was probably shoulder-deep, but he must have gone in head first.'

The cries at night in this street. A woman cried out just now loudly, it was silent before that, and it's been quiet again since. Just the sound of the occasional car still driving past along the main road. Two car doors slamming below. It's about one in the morning.

I try hard not to cry out, which is difficult on these rough stones with the water up to my neck, in a dream in which someone is talking at me, one of those commissars, one of my bad childhood memories, is questioning me, interrogating me, to and fro, about this, and then, all of a sudden, about that, and from whom and how and where and when. This cross-examination, am I going to resist it and the taunts of this madman who is hammering away at me like a doctor, trying to check my reflexes, for if you're normal and in the right you should also react normally, your muscles should contract instantly. The way he and his accomplices stand away from me and poke me, push me around with long poles, while I quickly curl myself up, draw my head and knees up to my body, grip myself with my arms, cut myself off from the world into a ball while they keep prodding me with their poles, no, I shout across to them, I won't say anything, no one is guilty, I don't know anyone here, no names, or only false ones, all I can do is name people who don't exist, I just want to go away, quickly, before it's too late, they can try and try but I won't save myself, won't hold on to their poles, stretched outwards like an offer of rescue, won't give up my position, curled into a balloon, which is keeping me afloat, I've still got some air.

'Being able to help people, it's a gift I've got. Even back in the days when I worked at the factory, when something happened, something went wrong, if there was an accident, I always had to get involved, I always had to help. I've still got the certificate the committee gave me. Of course it's good to help people, but they went too far, and then when they started saying things and then changing the story later, that was it, I stopped helping, I wouldn't stand for that!
Most people do piece-work so that they can earn more. There are some people who work slowly, but they're more con- scientious, and then there are the ones who just rush away,

who just want to get as much done as possible, and the results are sometimes really bad. Of course, you always get some people who can work quickly and well, you never get more than a handful of these in any group of people but they still manage to hurt others, the ones who work well but who aren't so quick. There's no point in discussing the bad workers, it's up to the boss to deal with them. Only, as a rule, the people who follow them have a hard time because of them, they're the ones who get the poor work passed on to them. They have to correct all the mistakes and that means if they're on piece-work they're not going to earn enough money. Piece-work has become a real menace. They introduced it so they could produce more but they didn't stop to think about the quality of the work. I don't know if they're still on piece-work, I stopped having anything to do with all that when I left work, I got out of it completely.'

I count the days: yesterday, nine, today, eight, I cannot do the work for the Federation of Swiss Architects, I think up a new excuse each day, the hours fly past and I stand around, wander around, load the washing machine, have something to eat, water the flowers, move the plants, do the ironing, listen to a record, watch Gian building kitchen shelves, hand him a plank, and find my own behaviour alarming, after all, there are people who can work quickly and efficiently. Occasionally, rarely, I too am one of those quick and able people, what I'm doing now can't possibly be real, can't be serious. Yet at the same time I know that the week I've got left is barely enough to produce a good piece of work. *My peace is shattered. I can see that what I was intending to do should not be undertaken like an exercise, at the last minute, like a piece of schoolwork handed in late, with a bad conscience.*

I remember a young graphic artist in New York, commissioned to design the Christmas catalogue for our workshop, and who described in colourful detail the work he had done in the past. Christmas came and he had barely started; the photos hadn't been plated, a lot of money had been spent, there was no catalogue. His behaviour, so like my own at the present, was incomprehensible to me then. I must not accept this kind of work again, the kind of task where the words, the sentences, vanish the moment I sit down at my typewriter. Because I'm losing a certain discipline, that pleasure in schoolwork.

'Yes, when I see someone's having a hard time, helping is just instinctive with me, it's in my nature, how should I put it, it's a gift not everyone's got. Just go right in and help. Moral problems, emotional problems, it's all the same, but not money problems, anything but that! That's thankless, that's the most thankless situation you can get yourself into. Because if you're helping people with their money problems they never stop to ask you how you are, they never ask whether you're in need of money yourself now, the moment they're back on their feet they just walk straight past you. That's where a lot of people make mistakes. As long as they're in difficulties they want to know you, but the moment they're all right again they just ignore you. That's how it is. It's rare to find anyone who's grateful, and it doesn't matter where you go, it's the same everywhere.

I could never understand what young Karl did. What made him do it? What suddenly happened to him was that he got greedy for money. The children really had a terrible time of it home. The father did go out to work and bring in some money all right, but he was always doing foolish things, which doesn't set the children a very good example. And he really had it in for the boy, he was always the one who had to pay for it when one of the other children got up to mischief, Karl always got the blame, and he often used to say to me: I'm going to get my own back on my father one of these days! That'll just show him what it's like to be tormented all the time. And that's what he did. But he'd stolen things before,

before he went to the kindergarten and his mother knew about it and kept quiet about it instead of taking the child to a doctor, to someone who knows what to do with a child like that. He became greedy for money because they took everything away from him, Sunday evenings when he got home: Hand over the money! money he'd got for working for me. I had him when he was even younger, I had him with me since he was eleven years old, for five years, until he was sixteen, that's when he did it. I gave him seven or eight francs for the Sunday afternoon at first. I was quite happy about it, he was a real help to me, he did the cleaning for me and everything. And later, when he was thirteen I gave him ten francs and when he was fourteen, fifteen, I gave him fifteen francs, maybe even sixteen, depending on my takings. If the takings were good he also had to work hard and if they weren't so good, I couldn't give him so much. And when he was sixteen and started his apprenticeship, I sometimes used to give him eighteen, twenty, twenty-two, and he often got tips as well, so he usually got four or five francs on top of that. But when he got home it was: Hand over the money! They took it all off him and if he wanted anything he really had to plead with them to get any. He came to me once and said: Frau Gerster, I've got no money, I can't buy anything. And he was so fond of sweet things, biscuits. So if he could earn anything he immediately gobbled it all up. He took the double windows down and carried them inside for nearly all the old people in my street, and he went shopping for them as well as the work he did for me, he did jobs for people when the weather was bad and they gave him something for his help, a franc here, two francs there, and I said to him: Put it to one side. But he was spotted when he went to buy sweets and he probably got into trouble at home. But I never worried about them, oh yes, they warned me to keep out of their affairs. His mother went away, she became ill in the autumn so he was with me most of the winter. She had an inflammation of the brain, that came from her character, she was a bit strange. She said "no" to

everything and it was always the children who had to suffer
for it when she didn't manage to get her own way, the children
just used to go off, run away from home, and her husband was
never up to any good either. Young Karl really started to go
astray when he was very young, especially sexually. I mean,
I'm sure he must have masturbated in bed, because he didn't
go chasing girls, not him, and I thought, my sister said the
same later, that he was over-intelligent, that's what he was.
And he had to get some satisfaction somehow, because he
suffered, he suffered a great deal psychologically, he's probably
still suffering now.

This is what I wrote for the lawyer: *His mother had been in
service, and her employers were very pleased with her work,
but she was one for the boys. She got pregnant. Otto wouldn't
marry her. Had to bear all the expense of having a child.
Walter then fell into the trap, married her, at the recruiting
school. Agnes and then Karl were born. Nothing to eat half the
time because Walter couldn't hold down a job. Moved to
Rorschach. No accommodation, left their furniture at the
railway station. Walter had bluffed, tried to buy a hotel or
restaurant when there was no money, had signed a contract
which his wife then managed to terminate with great difficulty.
He was bragging a lot, showing off. Wife and children suffered
greatly because of it. Walter went out drinking, often didn't
come home at night. Mother and father rowed a lot, children
suffered. Then got heavily into debt, bought a car, second hand.
Caused an accident. Had to pay up. Bought another car,
second hand, no money, old repairs not yet paid off. Tried to
buy a house with no money, all hot air, lies. Moved from one job
to the next, he always put the blame on someone else. And all
the time, when things were going badly at home, it was always
Karl who got the blame, he was the family scapegoat. For the
last three years the mother went out to work because a fifth
child had come along. As for the mother: the children were
always clean. She was a first-class housekeeper but the children
suffered a lot, she didn't treat them properly, if one of them did*

*something wrong, they were all punished. Unfortunately she
had this money sickness, took all their money away from them
whenever they made the effort to earn some. She was very hard
with the children, you never saw her showing them any
affection, all they got were slaps, boxed ears, never any
tenderness. And a lot of harsh words. For example: One
Mother's Day, Karl brought her some lovely tulips, to please
her, he'd bought them with the money he got from doing jobs for
people. But his mother wasn't pleased; the first thing she said
was: where did you get the money for those flowers, really
angrily, and this hurt Karl deeply, shattered all his pleasure,
and she took the flowers, crushed them and threw them into the
dustbin. Karl came over to us, tears streaming down his face,
and cried his heart out, saying over and over again: I'm never
buying flowers for her again, and then he told us what had
happened. Maybe something had just made her angry and you
came along at the wrong moment, don't take it to heart, she'll
soon see how silly she's been, my sister and I told him. And then
he told us that his father had been out all night, so she had
worked her anger out on the poor child, without thinking.* You
see, that's what I wrote down: "Case history of a broken
family." You can read it yourself and get a story from it. And I
really thought carefully about what I wrote down, it's very
different from talking.'

A student calls me, she wants to write an essay about one of
my books. I am helpless when faced by her questions about
the book and myself, how am I to explain everything? Things
that are incomprehensible to other people, but not to me. So
I refer her to articles and reviews. I answer like a lazy
schoolgirl who's only had time to skim through the book she's
being questioned on without having understood the first
thing about it, like someone who's never really thought about
themselves. A book I myself wrote and which is about myself,
among others. And what I wrote, which I thought out so
carefully, is not the same as talking about it.

'With this woman it was all because of her health, she'd strained her nerves, everything, and the body's left without any resistance. But you can't really say that it's fate, it's her own fault that she's in such a bad state now. I used to say to her sometimes: don't react like that, when she came down to the lake. I think I've already told you about what happened when the boy had just earned his first five franc piece, instead of thanking him, she gave him a clout, and that's a sign of bad character and egoism towards her own children. Everything depends on the way parents bring their children up. People who've got children but didn't really want them and who bring them up as if it were a duty and don't give them any real parental affection, people like that shouldn't have any children at all, I'm quite sure about that, I'm quite against it. There is such a thing as parental instinct, maternal instinct, with people who love their children and look after them, you'll never find anything like this happening to them, they couldn't do it.

When I had my little boy I stopped going out to work. I could have gone on, the boss asked me to leave the child in the crèche, he even offered to pay for it so I could continue coming to work, but I said: No, it's out of the question, if I've got a child I'm going to bring it up myself, not leave it to other people.'

After my children were born I too said: 'I want to bring them up myself and not leave it to other people.' I set up my work-bench at home and worked beside the cot or the playpen, next to the children as they played. The children started to copy my work and their father's work in the games they played from quite an early age, they modelled, hammered, did engravings, painted and drew.

'I was happy with my life, I was content, we had enough to eat in spite of everything, my husband did have a job, after all, and during the war he had to go away, he was in the war for over a thousand days, in the army, that is, from '39 to '43, and life had to go on. So I just managed as best I could. We moved here, I used to go out binding vines in the spring, I learnt that at school, when we were little we had to go out into the vineyards, and now and then I did some cleaning jobs, helped out in the guest house, anything that came along. If I just earned enough to buy food for my little boy and myself, my husband had to pay the rest. We didn't have much during the mobilization.'

In the summer, lots more children suddenly appeared here. There seemed to be twice as many as usual in the windows across the street. They've come to be with their parents during the holidays, my children inform me. They go to school in Italy, can't speak French and can't talk to their little brothers' and sisters' friends here.

'So for children it's extremely important that you bring them up to have a proper conscience, that you teach them what's right and what's not right so they can go on from there to learn it from life. That helps them a lot.'

Yes, these foreigners' children who aren't allowed to live with their parents all year round will have to learn all sorts of things for themselves.

'The other isn't necessary, religion isn't, but anyone who wants it should be able to have it. The only thing is that they start thinking the others aren't as good as they are. Anyway, I see it this way: what is our religion, our Church for? They pay priests, who have to study, for what? So why shouldn't everyone be united, why shouldn't we stick to what is given us at school, in childhood, what we were given then, why shouldn't we hang on to that? I mean, they didn't get me into the Salvation Army, my family used to go a lot, but not me, never, not even as a child. I only go to church very occasionally. But I always come out fuming about the sermon. It's not like it used to be, it isn't directed at your conscience. You can tell, it's just dictated, it doesn't come from the heart. I like a priest who speaks straight from the heart, without reading it, that's much more interesting, there's more point to it, not like the ones who have it all prepared beforehand. I suffered a lot from religion because there was a lot of bigotry, of sham piety at home, and that just isn't in me. We can't bring children up exactly as we were brought up. That's natural. That's the way of the world and there's not much we can do about it. It would be possible but not in a town, you have to live in the country for that, where they don't mix with other people as much.'

The children playing in the square round the fountain in which wine casks are sometimes left to soak, doesn't that make an idyllic picture? The fact that children can play so absorbedly among all the cars and workmen and people in the restaurants rather than in a proper playground with sandpits and climbing frames, proves it's an idyll. Unlike most of the children from other parts of the town, other towns, they can still see how the thread is cut on a water pipe and how sockets are joined, how roof guttering is bent, riveted and soldered, they observe curiously how central heating pipes and oil tanks are gas welded. They see 'here's how you do it for this, here's how you do it for that'; a machine spews out loosened horse hair, furniture is upholstered and mattresses stuffed. So the children are not only looked after by grandmother, mother or neighbour, with an occasional glance out of the window, the workmen know them too.

'But when they leave school, many children are very unsure of themselves, maybe they're not as grown-up as others, and they clam up. But you do get exceptions, and that's when you've explained things to them really thoroughly, no not sex, more about people and life, give them examples: Look, here's what you do for this, here's what you do for that, what do you think of it? I did that a lot with my children.

Like the time I showed my daughter how you get your bearings in a big town you've never been to before. I'd never been to Brussels before, either. So the first morning we went out I explained to Dorli: Now look, there's a big building over there, remember it! It was twenty-five stories high and had a big MARTINI advert on it, so I said to her: Remember what it looks like from this side and from the other side, and when you get into the city I'll bet you can still see the building from everywhere. And then we got a taxi — the taxis there were cheaper than the trams, the manager of the hotel we stayed at told us that, the Hôtel du Brabant or whatever it was called, I'd already had a word with him about what there was to do in the city, so we set off. We went to the Exhibition, you know, the place where the World Exhibition was held, as far as that, and we got out there and went to look at the, wait a minute, I've got it written down here, the Atomium, it really is enormous, gigantic, and we looked out from there and I said: Look, there it is, the Martini building, do you think we can find our way back? We'll walk back this afternoon, and we should be able to make our way straight to the hotel. We walked all through old Belgium, Brussels that is, and whenever we turned into a street we made sure we could still see the building and we were back at our hotel by about five. After that we made out a schedule and every day we took a taxi somewhere and made our way back on foot, and that's how you can always be sure of keeping your bearings. And it was good for Dorli. After two days in London, she lived a little way outside, she had to go into Town by underground, into London to do some shopping. It was quite a way to go, but she spotted something when she got to the station, a broadcasting tower, radio or something, and she made a note of it. She got a bit lost to start with because the streets all run in straight lines there, but then she spotted the tower and thought: I'll keep that tower in sight now and she found her way back to the tube station. After that she went all over the place and always found her way back safely like that.'

A journey sometime, somewhere. I imagine going to the Orient, in my mind's eye I can already picture one of those fairy-tale towns, like Fez, see myself in the bazaar, in the streets, in the peaceful, richly ornamented inner-courtyard of a mosque in one of those beautiful white or earth-coloured towns I know only from the *Thousand and One Nights* and from photographs. I've been planning a journey to the Near East or North Africa since I was sixteen years old, when I decided to become a silversmith just so I could go and live there. I imagined myself working in one of the workshops in one of the streets of one of those towns. Instead, I sat in a little workshop on New York's 54th Street. My daily walk from the Grand Central Station to work was easy to negotiate, all I had to do was keep R.C.A. VICTOR in sight; as everyone knows, in 'mid-town' New York all the streets run straight, parallel, and at the street corners the skyscraper could usually be seen between the other high buildings. I developed a system, designed to combat monotony, of inventing new zig-zag paths, as many variations as possible, one day turning left, that is, west, earlier before turning north again.

And then I'd sit there in the workshop for another day, sawing, filing, soldering, polishing, but in my thoughts, I was in a town like Fez, which, in reality, I've not yet seen.

I don't like departures, but I like the preparations for departures even less, all the tiresome arrangements, even for the members of the family who aren't participating in the journey, washing clothes, mending, tidying the flat, dashing about seeing to all the most pressing last minute business. But I do enjoy sitting in the train afterwards, the only part of a journey I enjoy is the travel itself. No responsibilities, no remonstrations. The further away from home I get, the more I can forget my work, enjoy looking out of the window, watching the countryside passing by and slowly changing, or I read, as we travel along: *I stepped hesitantly into the red of dawn, walked, searching for secrets, lost things, through the carriages.* Or I just sit, thinking of something or nothing, or I sleep. I could do without the arrival.

'It's bad here too, it's almost worse than in the town here. When they bring their friends home it's all right, but once you let them out — in other words you have to tell children: You may go out, of course, but behave properly, make sure people can see what you're up to, make sure people get a good impression of you. You have to talk to them a lot. Children of thirteen, fourteen, they're not like they used to be, we still used to be out playing at that age, but even in school now they discuss so many things, politics if they can, world affairs, and they criticize as well, if they can. Where we were saying at seventeen or eighteen: Look, she's doing this and she's doing that, they now start a lot earlier. They're really four or five years ahead of us at that age, intellectually. People kept a lot hidden from us, and we didn't have the newspapers either, maybe some rag or other, a family magazine. Now they've got television and all the journals which they can borrow, the children bring them home, the parents aren't bothered, you really should take notice of what children are given to read. Mine read a great deal, but what they read was right for their age. And then all this television, that's a big mistake, they find out all about it, and of course the parents don't steer them away from it and now they're even showing sexual films on television, it's crazy. I always say: it's crazy that children have to see all about something which is basically one of life's pleasures, but which is a private thing after all. Do you have to show children everything? They'll find out about it themselves soon enough.

I'm sure people were happier in the old days. There's no peace for anyone any more, not for children, not for anyone. And they're offered so much at school these days that they can't grasp it all, in one ear, out the other, and the brain stays as empty as ever. It used not to be like that, in the old days what the teacher told you went in and stayed there, for the rest of your life.'

Yes, they're offered so much at school these days, and there's no peace for anyone any more. He should ask himself, the pupil and the adult, whether he's an amateur or an expert, whether what he's been taught, what he's being taught now, is really the truth. 'What the teacher told you went in.' Is anyone accustomed to questioning his demands, his values, is he willing? Is anyone in a position to be able to do so? No, that 'stayed there, for the rest of your life. Do you really have to show children everything?'

We probably show our children 'everything' too early and so make their lives more difficult. But adults can be shown everything. The electrician would probably find the hundreds of visible coloured wires which lie intertwined like an intricate drawing on his switch panel as beautiful as a picture if the switch panel factory produced see-through covers. Just as he accepts, or is forced to accept the new see-through meters.

Just as I am forced to accept his grey plastic switch panel and the shape of the telephone, or rather one of the two choices offered us, and each of the boiler, fridge and radiator models offered us, or the excessive prices we have to pay for 'good design.'

I won't start describing the different noises made by all this machinery. I am forced to accept quite a lot of things I don't like, and when I realize just how many things there are in my house which I cannot, may not change, that's when the dissatisfaction sets in. If we were to move into a completed, rented flat there'd be even more things we'd have to put up with, we'd have to get used to. It's easy to understand why such disturbing questions are left untouched. They make you uneasy.

'Exactly, there's no peace for anyone today.

And people copy each other more today, that's got worse, it's quite bad today. And their character, it's up to you to shape that yourself, it's the way you treat them from babyhood that makes them what they are. Take my son, he went to England after he left school, and later his boss, it was a lady he'd worked for to improve his English, they have a lot of women bosses there, she said she wanted an *au pair* girl. And she thought: I had a boy who was very level-headed from a good family, very respectable, well brought-up, and I'm not saying this because he's my son, she just liked him, so she rang up about his sister and asked if she'd come as an *au pair*, and in five days it was all settled.

Dorli had left school and I wanted to keep her at home for a while so she could rest a little, she'd had a lot of trouble with her back: You must get right away from those school benches and we'll do some walking, I told her, walking did her a lot of good, we'll do a lot of walking for a while now and you can go on to do your training later, so she went away after training college, and I went with her.'

So, Dorli left home for the first time, well-guarded, accompanied by her mother who initiated the daughter into everything that was new and foreign to her, who carefully prepared her for anything she might encounter. After all, she had to set Dorli an example so she would know how to behave correctly.

'We worked out the cheapest way to get there, Kloten — London would have cost about 260, and how much was it by train? 75 francs. And she got a reduction because we told them she was going to be an *au pair*. So we went by train to Brussels, and there was a firm there offering cheap flights Brussels — London. And the difference between Kloten — London and the train journey we'd paid less for paid for my ticket to Brussels and back.'

The school benches didn't do my back any good either, but the hard work after I left school was even worse. And neither did my education at home or at school prepare me in any way for what I encountered afterwards, for what was to confront me. 'Behave properly, make sure people can see what you're up to, make sure people think you're a good person.' And as the Russians were daily getting closer and closer I was struggling with Latin and English, and with dates, the battles of the Seven Years War. Of course, a lot was hidden from us, much was badly explained, or rather, not explained at all, least of all sex. There wasn't any television yet, either. There was the radio, but the inflammatory broadcasts telling of atrocities which were used as a last, desperate bid to mobilize resistance, spread fear rather than advice about coping. We could learn that ourselves later, 'from life', which certainly does have a 'certain charm.'

'People were more considerate towards their parents then,' says Frau Gerster, 'cared about them more. People knew the hand that fed them.' No, at the end of the war we didn't even know that any longer. At the age of fifteen, just like an adult, I left my parents behind me and had to take on the responsibility of looking after my brother and sisters, only temporarily, thank goodness, and afterwards I had to decide all for myself what kind of school I should go to, what kind of profession I should train for. So before long my parents were no longer necessary, they weren't around, had dropped out of my life. I had to be independent, responsible for myself. From the end of the war, from the time with the farmers, then at the shoemaker's, my survival and the shape of that survival depended on my own actions. It could have worked out badly.

Later, in Zurich, leading an unaccustomedly peaceful existence, when there were no longer any immediate dangers to confront, this peace troubled me, it was difficult, often impossible to come to terms with order, to fit into an ordered lifestyle again. A year later, I was at the art college by then which was at that time the school which allowed the greatest freedom, my parents were with me again. With the same old ideas about education, the same demands and restrictions, no criticism or there'll be trouble, as if that whole period of self-reliance and dangers overcome had never existed, as if I was still just the child from a good family, the kind of well-protected young girl my grandmother had in mind, the last thing I myself wanted to be. There were the rows (yet maybe not all that many when I compare myself with my own children who are now about the same age), sometimes my brother and sisters and I managed with the greatest of effort, at my mother's request, to stop short of outright mutiny, out of consideration for my father's health, later, out of consideration for my grandmother's age. But, again, all this emphasis on showing consideration for others wasn't exactly what I needed to survive in New York.

Frau Gerster had friends in Brussels: 'who we met in Tessin, out in Teresete, we went there and there was this man who was bald and he never wore a hat or anything. We used to go out walking, sometimes we were ahead of them and sometimes we were behind, but one day, the further we went the nearer they got to us, until in the end they were level with us and we walked back to Teresete together, or whatever the place was called, and when we arrived they asked us to stay for a drink. And as we were sitting outside the bar the man collapsed, all of a sudden. I said: It must be sunstroke. They didn't know what to do, so I said: the best thing is to get some milk and soak some compresses in it. My husband dashed round all the farmhouses and eventually, much further up at a tiny hut, I can't remember the name of the mountain, they gave him some milk, they just had one cow. Twenty minutes went by and he still hadn't recovered; his wife was in a real state, and as soon as my husband got back we soaked bandages in the milk. And all of a sudden the man from Brussels opened his eyes and he recovered. I didn't give him Coramin, I did have some with me but I gave him valerian drops instead. After that we all took the train back to Lugano. They went to the doctor's, she told us when we met them again, we bumped into them, the people from Brussels, in Ponte Stresa, where you cross into Italy, he was a clerk at the law courts in Brussels, and they were overjoyed to see us, the doctor had told them they'd been lucky to find someone who knew what to do.'

Do I really enjoy these stories about a person who's always so ready to help, to whom helping is an instinct, a gift, and who's always making other people so happy, while I myself feel increasingly helpless as the stories go on? Even when I'm working, when I'm writing. It flows from my pen, or from my head through to my pen much better in the evening, at night, when it's too late, when I've got somthing else to do; at times like that I could write, can write, but it means I can't sleep, I go on writing instead of sleeping, even if it's only in my head. Because I'm missing that certain discipline, that sense of carrying out my duty. Which I almost regret.

Two shots outside. My watch has stopped, I don't know how late or how early it is.

My peace is shattered. No security, at least none as yet.

No protective peace, the constant noise from dawn until past midnight, and even in the remaining hours of darkness, often a cry of despair, and I can't tell if it's a cry for help, calling me, urgently, making sleep impossible.

The growing desire for peace, which gets more and more pressing. There are times when everything, all my composure, all my success depends on me getting some peace right now. Again and again my efforts are being thwarted, crushed.

Mademoiselle Alice loves garlic and cabbage, her kitchen smells rise right up to the top floor, fill the studio, it stinks like a latrine. The stench infiltrates the concentration which has cost me so much to achieve and eats it away like a corrosive poison.

'The doctor said he didn't know about that,' Frau Gerster's friends from Brussels had told her, 'about the milk. It's the best thing you can possibly do, cream, fresh cream is even better.

From then on they always wrote to us, told us what was happening at home and sent the children ten francs each at Christmas, and then my son went to see them on his way to England, he stayed with them a week. Later on I wanted to visit them with my daughter, I wrote to them, but there was no one at the station when we got to Brussels. So the first thing I had to do was find us a room. We got into a taxi and asked the driver to take us to a hotel, and he thought we were two whores, you see! So he took us to the biggest of the hotels where the prostitutes go. I said: I must see the room first, I must see the toilets, I wasn't at all keen on going inside but I had to set Dorli a good example, I had to show her the best thing to do. And you can imagine what the rooms were like! One was 80 frans for a night, another was 120 francs and another was 220, in that sort of hotel, so I told him, the taxi man, he waited while all this was going on, told him that this was no good, that I couldn't possibly pay those kind of prices, he wasn't to think that's what we'd come for, and where on earth did he think he was taking us!

Anyway, I had the address of a chap, Wollenberg, who used to stay here at the Hôtel du Lac quite often, and he always came down to the lake to see us. Wait a moment, I've got the address of that Wollenberg chap, we'll ring him up, maybe he can help us. And that's what he did, he told us to wait at the hotel we were ringing from while he came to pick us up, so we waited in the Paradise, the Paradise Hotel.'

The cries of fear or passion, or the frequent bursts of hearty laughter, echoed from across the street, more happy laughter, or arguments, rows, people giving vent to their emotions and in so doing arousing more, new emotions, ones which are foreign to me as well as ones I understand: I can sense my own pleasure when I'm feeling happy, and sometimes when I'm angry. An intense emotion being communicated, where

I was taught to dismiss it, to lock it up inside myself.

Where were we? In paradise.

Is it possible to pretend you don't care where you are or what your circumstances are? I don't have to like everything I hear, not even all the stories I should like. A lot of things here ought to please me, but I can't like everything, and some things can really incense me. Do the other people, the foreigners, like it here in this street? Sometimes life gets out of control. At weekends, on sunny afternoons, warm evenings. Cries mingled with laughter and singing and even conversations enter the flats through the open windows, so you get caught up in what's going on all around you, in a broader concept of living, no matter what you're doing; any isolated, hermetic existence is out of the question. Work is over, the sun streams in, Saturday afternoon, Sunday, holidays, a little freedom, short-lived, perhaps, but joyfully seized.

Frau Gerster had an experience with him too, once: 'with Wollenberg, when someone drowned and he helped us. That evening we were sitting together down by the lake, there were stones there before, just paved with stones, I can show you a picture of how lovely it was. The trees as well, when you look at those Japanese acacias down there now, they let the warmth and the heat through in summer, in spite of the shade, when it's hot you can be sure there'll be no one sitting under the acacias, people even move the benches to sit here.'

The lopped acacias and the plane trees with their gnarled, twisted branches, whose silhouettes remind you of Louis Soutter's later pictures: each one with a thin branch, a single finger which points sideways out of the thick swellings of the tree stumps, the ones growing upwards are chopped off so that with each year they grow further across to form a roof, a canopy. The pruned plane trees in front of the cantonal bank. Even the sadly mutilated poplar and birch trees down on the shore of the lake, near the bathing area, have had human will forced upon them and are now growing as they ought to grow. Young shoots are growing from the trunk of a chestnut tree in front of the station, I can feel someone telling me to break them off. But I don't want to. Oh, but the tree will look much better, my grandmother insists gently as we walk along a tree-lined avenue, not among the chestnut trees in the garden at home, but in a park in Bern, she goes from tree to tree and breaks off the pale-green shoots, full of sap, cleanly from the trunk, the 'wild shoots' she calls them. It must have been in the gardens of a home for elderly or convalscent lady teachers where she lived for a while; there was a very forceful lady in charge there, next to whom my grandmother looked so tiny, as if it was a children's home she was in.

'And that tree over in the centre, there used to be four like that, and as I walked down to the lake one day there were three on the ground, this was before they'd decided they wanted to chop the plane trees down as well, anyway, I dashed home and rang Bern to ask whether these trees weren't protected.

And they said: Yes.

So I said: Well they've chopped three of them down already and there's another one they also want to chop down. That was out of the question they said, would I wait a moment. And the tree's still there, that was a victory for me, the fact that it didn't go the same way as the others.'

I was in the cable car again last night, in a dream. And just like from the windows of the Liechtenstein's castle, I am looking out over a park filled with enormous exotic trees and a neglected old nursery. Now, down below, the gardener, like my grandfather, emerges from the high bushes, comes towards me and helps me look for the flowers I had spotted here and there from above. We walk down the sloping garden, along old walls, a high, ramshackle house and a dilapidated greenhouse and search around under the acacias among countless other kinds of plants. A lot of weeds between the bushes. When we at last find the pink flowers, the gardener says, no, those aren't the ones I meant, and I too realize that they are different flowers altogether. He digs a bunch of them up, mentions a name I've now fogotten, and gives it to me. But the blue flowers I'm looking for we don't find.

The way you dig, the way my grandfather carefully digs round a clump of tubers or onions or rhizomes with the trowel and then lifts the conical ball out of the earth and holds it so it doesn't fall apart, so the earth holds together. The love of what you're doing, understanding the meaning of every detail. My son Patrick used to plant flowers in a similar way when he was a little boy. And today, in exactly the same way, he builds a wall or can tell when the chimney he's building is true.

'Anyway, that night we stayed up with Wollenberg until about two in the morning, sitting by the lakeside, and suddenly a boy jumped into the water, and then he got a kind of cramp, that's when you've had a big meal, when you jump into the water with a full stomach, that's what you call cramp: when the heart stops because the stomach is too full of food.

Look, you can see from this photo how much nicer it was with the stones at the harbour. One morning, I was the first one to get my boats out on the lake, they tell me I have to move my boats. I certainly will not move my boats, I say, if you want them moved you'll have to do it yourselves. And when I came back down to the lake the boats were out of the water and they started putting concrete down and making steps, and no one had been told. At the same time they raised their prices from 15 to 60 francs, and they're still going up, you have to pay 90 francs now for a mooring. The prices went up and up, and you can imagine what I had to pay for four *pedalos* and the boat. And on top of that there was 330 for laying them up. So then I started taking a stand against them. Things do go wrong sometimes. You can't take everything to heart, or you'd never get anywhere, but you can say something.' She's right, you shouldn't lock everything up inside you, as I was taught to do, it doesn't get you anywhere, you can say something at least.

'And I told them, at the town hall. I kept going up there with the dog. And they don't tell me not to come back, oh no, they tell me not to bring the dog with me: He smells. And I gave him an answer all right, that fellow up there, that dog's a darn sight cleaner than your mouth! That's what he got from me!'

When we arrived here my younger children couldn't speak French yet. The first things they picked up were the words and expressions you shouldn't use. But what if people use them! the children protest, and all I can do is explain where and when you can't say this or that particular word. And I beg them not to try this French out on Mademoiselle Alice. They'd love to do it when Mademoiselle shows them how to wash the steps properly.

She's been showing tenants how to do this for years, but I fear that no Spaniard has ever done it as badly as we do. And we're always forgetting that it's Saturday. She says she knows all the tenants by their footsteps and if someone has left the light on in the corridor, she'll climb three flights of stairs to say: Monsieur Alvarez, it was you!

I also leave the light on. The inside of the building is a dark cave. The outermost rooms all have two windows, they're large and well-lit and perfectly habitable. When you close the shutters at night you lock the room onto the rest of the cavernous interior; you also lock yourself in when you go to bed, and yourself away from the street.

Mademoiselle Alice usually leaves her shutters closed during the day. At night she stands by her half-open window and watches the street.

Mademoiselle Alice's shiny polished wood, her bright, clean doorstep: the sign of an old spinster defying the dirt here, resisting the temptation of giving in to fresh dust which accumulates daily, the continuous progress of decay, resisting the temptation to let yourself go, go under.

Going the way of all things, all flesh, Frau Gerster would say: 'she's just extremely particular, is Alice.' The doorstep is as spotless as she is, like her crisply-ironed clothes, her hair, so perfectly arranged every day, her upright bearing. Even when she's ill. She's got asthma. It's her fight for survival, the dust really could kill her.

Her scrubbed, polished and shining stairs which I slipped on and fell down, a whole flight, scraping my spine along the steps after receiving a sharp blow on one kidney so I couldn't get up again and had to crawl up the stairs on all fours, like Gero, to my bed five flights up, in considerable pain, which dispells or replaces my angry thoughts and feelings.

I could blame Mademoiselle Alice and her cleaning, waxing and polishing of the stairs for my fall, just as Frau Gerster blames Karl, but I sooner console myself with my own inability to clean regularly and properly: Thank heavens! Otherwise I'd have slipped down two flights not just one.

'I took him out every morning, every lunchtime, every evening, even when the weather was bad. He always, always carried his stone. He used to fetch pieces of wood as well, you couldn't stop him. I collected all the planks and twigs, all the wood that floated to the shore, and when he saw it he went and fetched the whole lot. When he saw a stick he would jump off a wall five foot high to fetch it, he was always the same, he even came to me once, this is when we still had a wood stove, with a plank which was about eight metres long, two centimetres thick and thirty centimetres wide, we always wondered why on earth he did it. And once, when I was over at the island with the boat the boy let him off the lead, and all of a sudden he was gone, he'd swim after me and was two-thirds of the way there. They went out and caught him, he was almost worn out. He was a good swimmer, and a diver. I had to keep my eye on him, sometimes he did a belly flop and I was afraid he might burst his insides, they like doing that, splashing with their bellies, but the water has a great resistance.'

When I start I just plunge straight into my work, I've already got something nicely worked out, I like doing that, lying there at night, getting things all carefully planned. Sentences and whole stories, and now I'm hitting my head against . . . what? If it's not a brick wall, it's paper. Resistance. I must be careful, am afraid that everything is going to burst any minute now, language has a resistance.

And when Frau Gerster was in a bad way because of her husband 'then he would come up to me and ask me, beg me to take him out, so I just had to go out, they're very sensitive about someone you would say is "down" or unhappy, they're very sensitive then, much more than usual, when you're feeling all right. Yes, they take your mind off things because you take them out for walks and they comfort you by making a fuss of you, you can see it in their eyes, you see it from their heads when they sit next to you, from the expression on their faces, you can see what they're trying to do, if you spend time with them.

But psychological matters are quite different. When you can't find fault with a person about anything, when he's not bad, when he doesn't do anything bad, when he only ever does good, when he's cheerful, that's all to do with character. It's wrong to have children and look after their physical needs but to neglect their minds, their intellect, they'll be empty then, and it's a terrible shame if you do nothing for their souls. There was a woman down at the lake once, she'd adopted a Vietnamese child, and he fell over and cried because he cut his knee, of course it hurt on those stones. He started to cry, looked at his knee and went on crying. But the maternal instinct wasn't there, the woman had never had a child of her own, I mean, I would have picked the child up and given it a cuddle, stroked it and said: All better now. But nothing. So I said to her: Of course, the poor little thing's missing it's mother. You don't know the first thing about that child, it's an emotional thing, you'd certainly never have been given a child if I had anything to do with it! You can mollycoddle a child, pamper it a bit if you like, anything but that, it really upset me, I felt like taking it away from her. Every child has a soul. True, there is such a thing as a bad soul.'

I know now that the little fair-haired boy across the street is called Augusti, he's plucked up enough courage to come as far as our corridor now. Our children are painting sailing boats and blue waves on the old oil painted walls. I give Augusti a brush, but he'd rather watch the girls.

Well I wouldn't paint on the walls in someone else's house, either, says Carolina.

Augusti! Augusti! A young woman you only ever see in the evenings and at weekends leans far out of the window.

He's with us!, Martigna calls over to her.

I also know exactly which tune comes after which on the tape belonging to the neighbours who live to our left on the second floor. That tape, the bane of my life. There must be cracks in the wall beneath the wallpaper in my room.

'And then there are the kind,' says Frau Gerster, 'who manage to infuriate everyone somehow, like the boss; my husband had an argument with him, about something he couldn't do anything about. I could have taken action against the boss, but there was no point in it. The boss plagued countless people, the older ones who'd worked there quite a long time, those were the ones he used to plague, my husband was the last one, so he started on him. He didn't let it bother him too much, he just got on with his work, but somehow, towards the end it always seemed to be my husband who got all the dirty work, the oldest one always got landed with the worst jobs. And he took all this so much to heart, he bottled it all up inside him and kept it to himself, until eventually he had this spasm, and that was it. Friday morning at about eight o'clock. It's like a stroke but they call it an intrax. It's not the same as an infarct, either, they come from the blood circulation, his was a spasm. Anyway, the man he worked with looked over at him, he had a screwdriver in his hand and it fell to the floor and my husband fell slowly, collapsed like a concertina and scraped his face along the edge of the table which was covered with metal, he was all scratched. The other man thought he was trying to pick the screwdriver up, but when he saw the way he just collapsed he said to himself: something must be wrong. His head on the floor and all blue, all blue immediately. They took him to hospital and they found that's what it was. The doctor himself hadn't been able to understand it.

Anyway, the workers there didn't want to tell me what had happened, none of them, so there was trouble! I kept on and on asking questions, and even now, fourteen years later, when I met the foreman recently, he went quite white when he saw me, he couldn't pretend he didn't know what it was all about.'

I find my own complaining idiotic. And I don't understand it, don't understand myself.

'They don't help each other, the workers don't, because they're jealous of each other, when one of them earns a bit more than another they get jealous and that's what's so crazy about the whole thing. When they go on strike, that's when you can see things as they really are, there are some who are a bit more intelligent than the others and they start the strike. The type who wants to get somewhere, he'll watch, but not just for himself, he's not an egoist, and the others, the ones who only care about their money, they send him along and they'll stand by him for a while because they don't want to be the ones to stand back, but they won't actually help, oh no, they won't go along themselves, never, they won't back him up, they'll leave all the talking to the one who can do the talking. And that's where the ones who are more intelligent, the ones you can talk to, that's where they can make something of themselves, but the others, they never get anywhere, yet they grumble all the same, and they get jealous: he'll get to the top all right! But they never go along to help him out, he has to do it all himself! After a certain point everyone's on their own, it's each for himself, because of this egotistic streak they've all got inside them.'

Frail little Augusti, playing by himself or with the pigeons he attracts by putting food on his hand. If I were to go into the little boy's history I'd find out about where he was born, what his parents did, a few dates, a few more details about his life, past and present. But it's not a question of writing stories or drawing conclusions from what I see. Just what I see tells me more: The picture of the little boy attracting the pigeons with his outstretched hand while his grandmother sits next to him, busy sewing something that's not for her, not inside the room, isolated from the outside world, but at the open window where she can see what's going on, even notices me and nods her head in greeting. We've been saying hello to each other for months now, we sometimes exchange a few words, it's as if I've always known her, as if she brought me up, like she's bringing up her grandson, for she reminds me of my grandmother.

She really does look very like her, says Gian.

Augusti could become a story now, the scene is already in the past.

It's got cold and I haven't looked out of the window properly for a couple of days. In spite of the cold, the windows of the flat belonging to the two young Italians are open. I look across every day now, they're always open, the shutters swing in the wind and the room behind is dark in the evenings. No more *bel canto*.

The shutters of the ground-floor flat are also closed now, night and day.

I haven't seen the little girl who spits for weeks.

They've all gone, says a child from the same building: no, they're not coming back.

A VENDRE. The building is for sale; the child and the last of the tenants have also disappeared now.

'Everyone wants to be good, but no one's prepared to make any sacrifices when it comes to it. If I was younger and I knew what I know today, I'd do a few things differently too. But I'd never get mixed up in politics.'

Why?

'Because anyone who gets involved in politics is finished.'

How do you mean?

'Because in politics you've mainly got people who don't say what they mean; when that one's doing well you help him, and when the other one's doing well you help him. But you'll never find anyone, not a single one of them who'll ever say: Fine, that's the policy we're going to stick to! You should support what is right, what's good, something that'll get you somewhere, in one way or another, but you mustn't waver. If you're dealing with dishonest people it just won't work.'

Because I'm younger and because I know a lot of the things I do not like, things which appal me, cannot be changed by people on their own, by individual efforts, I feel I should do something different. Get involved in politics.

'You've got too few people with good ideas who are prepared to speak their minds, you've got too little backing to be able to say what you think. Of course it would come in time, but it's an art. Take that fellow Weber, the one from Montreux or Vevey, who goes all out to make sure that things don't get spoilt, he started off in a small way and now he only deals with big issues, but he should still be backing smaller campaigns, I'm going to write to him about it again. I asked him about the trees, and he told me to get my gun and shoot them down, then they'd soon stop.

So I told him that wasn't what I was asking, I was asking about the moral issue, and couldn't he help me. He's helped many people in Switzerland, but he arrives too late sometimes, when things are already moving. He has done some good. Now he only gets involved in big issues in Africa and Canada.

Why don't more people do that sort of thing? Because they don't want to be the ones who get misjudged by people and who don't get enough support.

Things do go wrong sometimes. But I didn't care, they used to call me "The Viper" sometimes. Yes, I really would give them a talking to, really speak my mind, I always do that, in the past I've certainly told people what I thought of them, but they've still come back, they respect you for it. But there's no point in carrying on if you don't have confidence, if you don't believe: I can do it! Some nights I didn't sleep because of the trees. I used to wonder: can you manage it or can't you manage it? And I always told myself: It'll work, it must, it must work. And some mornings I woke up feeling quite uncertain, many people, even council officials told me: You'll never manage it! It's a waste of time. But I said to them: You look after your affairs and I'll look after mine, but I'll also look after the trees, not just for myself but for all the people of Seewyler and for the foreigners too.'

Describing another human being, which is what I've been trying to do for so long with Eliette and which I never seem to manage, perhaps because I myself am getting in the way, suddenly doesn't seem so tortuously difficult, quite the contrary. (Eliette, although she's not me, always turns out like a self-portrait). Frau Gerster is so totally incompatible with me that there's no chance of this becoming another self-portrait, even if she does, like myself, derive great pleasure from going to a play or exhibition (it doesn't necessarily have to be Rubens for me) and does borrow books from the public library. Describing a person who's my complete opposite, or letting her describe herself, is fun. And I think I can manage it. I notice the way she leads me away from myself and my own difficulties and highlights other matters, to which my reaction is often: fine for her, but not for me, no, it wouldn't work. I'm not interested in 'getting on', and unlike Frau Gerster I'd be no use to the police, my face doesn't even inspire confidence like hers does. So she shows me my place in life: You look after your affairs, I'll look after mine. She helps me recognize my own position, helps me gain a deeper understanding of myself, however much I can also learn from what she tells me, however much, or rather because Frau Gerster causes me to question myself.

'Anyway, when I was having a hard time of it, because of my husband, Gero would come along, and I'd talk to him as if he were a human being. And that winter when I was working at home and when he could see I was depressed, he kept going backwards and forwards between me and the door until I got up, until he'd got me worked up so I had to go out.

There must be some kind of force that guides you, otherwise why is it that I was right there, where I could see the woman. I'd just gone out with the dog and had come round past the building merchant's when I saw her up there on the railway track, but she was a bit, well, a bit simple. She lived here, in the next street. And she lay down on the tracks and I dashed up there and was able to pull her clear, I certainly hadn't got her far from the tracks before the train came along. And it was an express, but I managed to get to her in time. Then I brought her home with me, her husband, Richard, he was away, so I kept her here until he came home. And then she got treatment, she's, how should I put it, extremely simple. Apparently her parents were desperate to marry her off so they put adverts in the paper. He came from Vevey, his mother had died and he was looking for someone to marry. She had lovely handwriting and he just went for her handwriting, and she seems very nice, kind-hearted and nice, and at the time he wasn't very observant and he married her; she kept the house nicely but the longer they were married the more serious her illness became and it became more and more obvious that she wasn't quite normal. She used to walk along sometimes, we always watched her, she used to run along, and she'd take two, three steps forward, then two, three back, once more, so you could see she wasn't normal. Richard got a divorce then, he got the divorce, because if he'd known she was ill he wouldn't have married her in the first place; he got the divorce because she kept it from him. No, no children, he was clever enough to know that. Yes, now how old was she when she got married? At least thirty-six, thirty-seven. And he must have suited her and she was able to get herself under control enough so he wouldn't notice anything. Richard was too inexperienced, he'd been at home most of his life, always helped out at home, he wasn't away long enough to notice that kind of thing. He still lives here.'

Here, everyone sees everyone else, people notice almost everything.

Many years ago we found ourselves a place to live, a lonely barn in a meadow above the Silsersee, but we didn't take it; the place was too beautiful and it cost too much to get the drains and electricity connected up. Since then, other people have also fallen for that meadow. I heard how the first person to build there, in Surlej, got worked up about the second person to come along. And it must have been the same for the second, the third and all the others who came and built new houses (and what houses!) right under their noses, who blocked their view. It can't be any fun living in a place where everyone's getting worked up about his neighbour, whom, or rather, whose house he only sees from the back, the toilet, bathroom, kitchen, staircase windows.

In our street everyone sees his neighbours from the front, anyone can talk to anyone else any time if he can speak French or Italian, Spanish or German, but you don't have to talk because everyone knows there's work to be done. Everyone knows eveything about everyone else, more or less, and everyone knows, I know:

the noise of the dustcart: it's either Tuesday or Friday, eight a.m. From the noise late at night in front of the 'Au Progrès' you can tell what kind of a party is breaking up and that it's Saturday night. And the loud conversations on the terraces mean it's Saturday or Sunday morning and good weather, onions at 10 a.m.: also Saturday or Sunday, but maybe rain.

Since the weather's turned cold it's been quiet on the terraces and it's also been quieter in the street in the evenings. Sometimes you really can believe you're living in the Canton of Bern. The smell of fish from the square, that's egli fish fillets at 13 francs at the 'Au Progrès'.

I will have to ignore a great deal of the information that penetrates my nose, my eyes and my ears to be able to live here, to find life here bearable, pleasant.

The report I've written for the Association of Swiss Architects is lying around. I've had everything worked out for a long time but it wasn't until last night, four o'clock this morning, that I actually got it finished. And I have to present it at nine:

Some writers have been commissioned by the architects to look at the question of the future, to look ahead. I don't know whether or to what extent this is necessarily a task for authors, I myself have avoided it, I can only bring to life something I know, can only attempt to reconstruct using words; futurology is not within my scope. By observing the present and comparing past experiences with new ones, by picking out a few details from the mass which surrounds me so I can sketch one tiny segment of a reality, I get to understand that reality better. What I try to describe isn't a model which points to the future, it's a mode of living which isn't even modern any more, an anachronism, even if there are similar streets with similar, maybe even identical social structures in many old towns. And many positive aspects of life here emerge from it, as well as the many sad ones, positive aspects you don't find in other parts of the town these days. If I was an architect or a planner I would see how I could impart something of this into a modern area. Since I've been living here I've started looking at new developments and suburbs from this angle, how their inhabitants co-exist.

'He still lives here, Richard does. He got married again, a very nice wife, a good marriage and it's going well, but I don't know, there must have been something wrong with him, something missing. I've known him, Richard, since he was a child, ever since he was born really. His mother used to come to market, they were from Alfermée, she brought him with her and I used to look after him while she was at the market. If I'd wanted to I could really have taken her to the police, but because I knew her, his first wife, that is, I thought there was no point in it, it's difficult enough already. They put her in a home, I expect she's still there.

And you could see it coming, she'd got it all planned. No doubt about it. She told me herself — how was it? I'm going to put an end to it all! Sometimes we used to discuss moral problems, down by the lake, there are quite a lot of people who come down to me at the lake, and she said to me, if she'd known what it was like to be married, she'd never have got married in the first place because her illness, the fact that she wasn't quite normal kept getting in the way, and her morale was really low.'

Why was it that Frau Gerster happened to be standing there just then, I wonder as I'm sitting in the train, would I have spotted the woman, would I have realized immediately what she was about to do? A well-dressed, middle-aged man with short hair and a little moustache in the middle of a round, red, self-satisfied looking face is walking along between the tracks a good way off Biel Station. He walks very upright, something I find impossible, his head, his shoulders thrust back, as if he has thrown the top half of his body back in pride, in a gesture of confident challenge, while I on the contrary, usually let my head and body slouch. I wonder what that man can be looking for between the rails, he's not wearing blue overalls nor the luminous red of the railway workers and I'm afraid, Frau Gerster's stories won't leave me in peace, that the man might have something in mind. Perhaps he's thinking of lying down on the tracks, throwing himself under a moving train. That wouldn't be in keeping with the impression he would make on a casual observer. On the other hand, this behaviour could be calculated to allay the suspicion of any possible observers, to enable him to carry out his plans undisturbed.

I'm getting like my grandmother who always expected the worst until it really happened. No. I can see the man continuing further, in my mind's eye I see him climbing down the railway embankment, making his way to safety.

'One year we had a whole spate of them; everyone who had problems, absolutely anything at all, simply went out and killed himself. But I was still at school then. In '23 or '24 we had eight suicides one after the other. One of them was the brother of Wälchli from next door, I can't swear to it but I would imagine that they had a row at home and he went out to the shed, took some cheddite in his mouth and set fire to it, it's like dynamite, the same kind of thing, that's where the crack in the wall comes from. Only not so many people used to pass through these courtyards in those days, it really used to be just a back-yard with the fountain, the farmers used to store all sorts of things there and we used to say: we're not going in there, it's dangerous, we hardly ever used to go through these courtyards or the passage between the houses when we were coming home from school, the most we ever did was to play marbles round the fountain sometimes, where it's nice and flat, but in general it's very dark there towards evening, it's not lit and it's rather spooky.
We heard the explosion right up at the school.
And then we had another one, where old Gribi's got his machinery warehouse now, one of the Oppikofers, that was

another family that used to fight a lot. The first or second of those samples fairs was on at the time and he told his wife he was going there, they lived separately, she was on the second floor and he on the first floor, and she thought, fine he's going off on his own again, he's off, and she didn't notice a thing, not even when five days had gone by. It was hot that summer and there were big flies everywhere and she finally thought: something's wrong, he hasn't come back and I can't get into the flat. The police came with a ladder and climbed up from the front and broke a window pane and found him hanging there.

And then at the same time we had a woman drown herself, but she was a depressive, and there was a fellow who hanged himself up in the woods, there just seemed to be a regular epidemic of them that year.

And then there was another one, two in fact, the first one slashed the veins in his wrist, but they caught him, and the second time, I can't remember what he did the second time, I think he cut his throat, and the third time he slashed his stomach with a scythe, the kind you use for grass, he sharpened it first, then a quick thrust, and that was it.

And the other one did the same thing, they copied each other, in the bar across the way, all of a sudden someone said, the barmaid said: Look, that's blood dripping down there, isn't it? and then he suddenly collapsed, didn't cry out or anything.

And then there was another one, but this was much later, across the street where the butcher is now, he hanged himself with a straw. I think he just wanted to find out, but not seriously, what it was like to hang yourself, he hung himself on the bannisters, just at body height so he could almost reach the ground so that, just in case, he wouldn't fall far, but it caught his adam's apple. With a straw, the kind you use to bind vines, they're made of barley or oats which they don't allow to ripen; they cut and dry them, then you wet them again and you can use them to bind things, you make a loop, you wind it round and pull, like that.

Yes, there've been any number of them, of that kind of person round here, but after all in such a small place you see everything, you hear everything. In a city the police are called, the person's taken away, and that's it, you can have people living in the same building who don't get to hear about it, but it's not like that here. In those days particularly Seewyler was like one big family, if anyone was in trouble we all helped him out. But these were ones who locked everything up inside them, they didn't go and tell anyone what was wrong, you sometimes heard them quarrelling, like all families, but no one thought they'd go that far.

Even in those days farmers had a hard time of it, they paid them very badly, and they weren't taking many people on in the factories either, and then the unemployment followed. It was already beginning to show its effect then. But that's not really why they did it, it was more of a fixation they had which they simply couldn't get out of their heads when they were really low.'

With dismay I remember and weep. You could have seen it coming, I tell myself, too late again, I can't forgive myself for not having noticed anything. But I didn't want to reckon with the worst happening, I didn't want to think about it at all, that it might go so far, optimism is often easier. He'll get over it, I thought, mistakenly, otherwise I might have been able to prevent a death.

'And in the old days, because of all the alcohol, they used to have children who were, well, you really have to call them idiots, it was the alcohol that did it. There were a lot of them in those years, they had no future, no job prospects, they wanted to do the same as everyone else but they couldn't manage it, some of them even wanted to get married. There was one of them who used to come down to me at the lake every Sunday for years. His sister used to give him pocket money so he bought a beer sometimes, but he couldn't take it. So his sister used to say to me: Look after him well for me. But I was glad to have him around.'

Why?

'Because Karl couldn't do just what he wanted to do, and

the other boys couldn't either. He, Charlie, used to feel like the boss when I wasn't around, but he didn't bother the boys at all, he just kept them on their guard. He used to enjoy coming to see me, I never turned him away, no one ever had any time for him, but I always did. Of course we had enough of him sometimes but I just used to tell myself: Let him do what he wants to do because it makes him feel: I've got someone here who trusts me, I am someone after all.'

How much longer can we go on like this? How much longer can Gian go on working like this? I want a rest, so do the children, they want to get out, they miss the garden, I miss it as well. There are six of us crowded together in this flat, the centre of which is like a building site, we sleep in noisy rooms on mattresses on the floor, we all cook, eat and wash in the dingy little kitchen. And get on each other's nerves. Discussions about how something should be done, arguments, shouting. We often quarrel. Truce! Our nerves are on edge, I beg for a suspension of hostilities, we've simply worn ourselves out, let's have some peace, take it easy, we've got no resistance left.

In such a small town people notice when you're on edge, when your spirits have reached rock-bottom, people hear. You can hear us right up at the Place de la Liberté. Such a lovely, hopeful name.

'I used to give Charlie a packet of cigarettes now and then instead of money, I wasn't allowed to give him that, for alcohol, because then he'd go off. He knew I valued him, no one else valued him, not even his sister valued him, not for all the weeks of work he did for her in the vineyard. She'd never have dreamed of going out for a walk with him in the evening, of course not, but when she was out he used to get himself blind drunk and then he'd turn nasty, naughty. He died quite suddenly, that upset me for a long time. He was sixty-eight, maybe seventy, a really little man. He came to us for many years, a good twenty, thirty years, so we really missed him, he'd been a real friend, Charlie had. Other people often came along and taunted him and when he was with me he could answer them back. Everyone, even the farmers used to come and tease Charlie. The way he used to come along wearing his cap and greet us: May I? he'd say. Yes, I'd answer: you're very welcome. I never went to his house, I mean, I never wanted it to look as if I was running after Charlie.

My old schoolfriend Ernest comes to see me sometimes now, his sister's died. We never used to talk much unless we happened to meet on the street, but he pops in sometimes now, when he's feeling a bit low, or he has his heart trouble. I can't turn him away, I can't do that, if he enjoys coming here what can I do?'

Eliette, the one I really wanted to write about and who got lost somewhere among all the new experiences I've had here, seems to have come back. Just when I thought I'd lost sight of her completely, she's turned up again.

Last summer was too hot. We had arranged to send the children to their grandmother's for the holidays so that we could go on working. Gian wanted to get as much work as possible done on the house and I wanted to get Frau Gerster's story finished. And then the hot weather came, unbearable for us, we'd been living in the mountains too long, so we just packed up and left. Just a break, time to breathe again.

And far away in a remote place I came across my old story which I thought I had long since forgotten, abandoned. In my mind's eye I saw Eliette sitting there in the old nursery, among my old things.

May I? she greeted me. What was she looking for here, in this place I left so long ago and had just rediscovered?

I just wanted to remind you of the good times we had. She's laughing: No point in moping, she says, you can always make the best of any situation!

Don't give me that story about things being better in the old days! And you don't even belong in this place, in my early childhood, our good times, the ones you represent, started in

Zurich. But it's all my imagination. I feel strong enough for several stories, several characters. Yes, I say, you may stay. When we got back I found I was able to concentrate on her for a few weeks, for about thirty pages I tried to continue my original work, tried to explain what Eliette stood for, but in doing this I interrupted my work with Frau Gerster. I often do that, it happens all too easily that one piece of work is thwarted by another. So now I'm trying to distance myself from Eliette and Eliette from myself again. She'll have to be patient. I hope she'll wait. Perhaps in the meantime she'll translate the Russian newspaper articles for me and the writing on the back of Madame Serova's photos and pictures. Sjerov, Serov, or Sierov, it's a good name. Ludmila Vladimirovna Serova. The husband's name would be Vladimirovitch, Alexandrovitch etc. Because he take's his father's name it is, of course, different from that of his wife, writes Eliette.

'I don't see much of him any more, the husband of the woman who lay on the railway line, Richard, I don't even ask about her because he's got another wife now and everything's going well, or rather I thought everything was going well. One day though, when I got off the train with Anna, that's the second wife, there he was at the station, she didn't expect him to be there, he hadn't realized she'd be on that train and she said to him: Come on, why don't you come home with me now. No, he said he still had some shopping to do, places to go. And as I turned into my street I saw him going into the bar across the way: So that's where you do your shopping these days, is it! I said: Richard, you really should have gone home with your wife just now, you shouldn't be going to the pub the moment you finish work, after all I had known him since he was a baby. But I'm not surprised when I hear people saying they're going to get divorced. And he was brought up close-fisted, mean, he's the sort of person who doesn't like giving anything away, yes, mean, that's the only way to describe him. And perhaps she's spent a lot of money, could well be, she used to be a secretary, could be. Anyway, as I've known him since he was a child I said to him: Just think a minute, you've got a wife and children now, you have to consider your family responsibilities you know, you've got a good life going for you now, why do you have to spoil it. No idea they were getting a divorce, but I did have a kind of feeling. It really upset me!

My husband never went to the pub, or if someone asked him along, he always said: I'll go and fetch my wife, he'd never have gone to the pub without his wife. I had to drop what I was doing when he called me and said: Come and have a cup of coffee. Dropped everything and went along with my husband, even if it exasperated me sometimes, but you have to go! With some people it's one thing, with others it's something else, you just have to put up with it, everyone's got his own little ways. Some people like going out in boats, my husband did, so I went along too; before we got our boats I used to be out on the lake with him every Sunday right through the summer, although if I'd wanted to I could have said: I want to go somewhere else. Then, that winter I said to him: Look, I'll decide what we do one Sunday and you can decide for the next Sunday and sometimes the children can say where they'd like to go. He used to say: we're going to Gaicht. We'd take a picnic with us and when we'd got there and were sitting at the roadside eating, the children would say: See, it's father's Sunday again!'

Our children usually tell us where they want to go: When I'm here I always want to go to the Engadine and when I'm there I always want to be here, says Carolina, the youngest.

We're all a little homesick for our old home, like all true Engadiners, homesick for the leafy views, the garden, the Piz Murail, the Corn Vadrett, the Rosatch, even I, the only one who didn't grow up there. I remember the roses by my desk in my room, which flowered at Christmas in the intense sunlight, all through the winter sometimes. I fear, I hardly dare admit it, that the good times are over. As if I were going under, in slow motion, irresistibly, like the grey light which is slowly fading here in the studio. An age-old sadness which reminds me of the same hour of the day, the same fears I knew as a child.

Up in the studio Gian is painting over sheets of newspaper, NOVOYE RUSSKOYE SLOVO, covering them with white paint so he can draw on them. On newspaper after newspaper, over the articles and titles and adverts which show through, he draws rows of skulls, animal skulls, mainly sheep, a series of drawings of a marten's skull, skulls unmistakenly drawn by him, by Gian, a series of self-portraits. Only the odd word of newsprint can be made out here and there: *The quintessence of modes of thought among Soviet youth, typewritten journal, monthly, no circulation, by a group of young intellectuals, liberal socialists, published since the days of Khruschev.* And: Neo-fascists from the Russian viewpoint. Something about a wedding. The last part of the serial 'Madame in the carriage'. *No rise in car prices. McGovern at meeting for the defence of Soviet Jewry. Military scandal in Bonn. The Ingrian hussars announce with deep sorrow the death in Toronto of their commanding officer, the Georgian cavalier Georgy Petrovitch Gursky.* Above this, a skull. Gian draws himself without hair, the self-portraits could be of someone else. Or someone could say: That's Georgy Petrovitch, I recognize his face. Someone clearing out this house one day might say: That must be Monsieur Serov, who else could it be? You can read, with difficulty admittedly, that in the Serovs' time Angela Davies is being awarded a medal in Moscow by the Soviet government, on the occasion of Lenin's centenary. This reward, says Angela Davies, is the greatest joy of her life, she will continue to act in accordance with the teachings of Lenin. The 31st August 1972. Was Monsieur Serov still alive then? That's him, I recognize his face, those are his features exactly, someone will say, perhaps.

'Yes, trust helps a lot, even my face is a big help. There are many people who come to visit me down by the lake and they know nothing will go any further. If people can be sure of that they'll come and tell you their problems. The times people have said to me: And what do you think, Frau Gerster? But you have to be philosophical about it and you have to accept that the answers you give can be right or wrong and that what you've said can sometimes be put to bad use without you meaning it like that, you meant well when you said it. You can never tell, other people see things differently, think differently. You might paint a picture and think it's beautiful, but someone else will think it's ugly. And it's just the same with talking and thinking and all that, no matter how hard you try.

Philosophical is . . . how should I put it, you never get two cases the same. Yet somehow you've got a firm basis to work from. Most people like us, though, who have never been taught anything about it, who've never been taught to think like that, they can't keep up, they don't understand things. And that's bad, in my opinion. Everyone's different, that's life, and you have to let people be themselves, but of course there's still the question of right and wrong.

When they came to tell me what had happened, the manager and the head of the office and someone else, the head of personnel, all three of them came. They asked our local policeman how they should go about it, so it wasn't too much of a shock. So Matthieu came down to the lake, he's our policeman, and he said: Frau Gerster, would you come with me, there are three gentlemen here to see you. But two or three days earlier my husband had said to me: Listen, don't get alarmed, they'll be coming to search the house soon, they want to go through all the houses to see if we're bringing anything home from work, there's a lot of stealing going on. All right? So I said: Let them come! Anyway, so when Matthieu came and said three gentlemen were there I told him I knew all about it and that he was to let them in, because he knew where I kept the key. But he said no, I had to go myself. So I went up to the house with the men, Matthieu in front, and I told him all he had to do was go into the living room, he knew the chest with my husband's tools in it was next to the piano, he could go and look, he'd never brought home a single nail or hidden a single screw. And then they told me they knew that, but they had to do it, you see, and all the way up here I was still thinking they had come to search the house. We went into the front room and I saw our policeman with tears streaming down his face. I said at once:

What's happened? Has something happened to my husband?

None of them dared say anything.

Has something happened to my husband?

And one of them said: Yes.

An accident?

No.

So I said: Then he's had a stroke, because of the state he got into yesterday. That Thursday evening he'd come home and said: I got into such a state at work today, I had this terrible pain all down my arm. So I said: That doesn't sound too good, you'll have to go to the doctor. And on Friday morning I said to him: Don't go to work. It doesn't make any difference whether you start early on Friday or Saturday, it doesn't mean we'll have any more money at the end of the year. Let them complain, just let them, he can do it himself, you stay at home.

But he said to me: No, I'm all right. Why should I miss a day, we'll only pay later. He didn't earn very much you see.

I think you should stay at home.

No, I'm going, I'm all right, it's gone now, and there you are, he was gone by quarter to eight! When he started work at seven o'clock they had a row, he probably told him what to do and my husband got cross, probably, they had an argument. And afterwards, when I asked the gentlemen if it had been an accident, they said:

No, much worse.

So, I said, he's had a stroke. Just tell me what happened and don't make me, I mean don't force me to guess. Just tell me the truth! So then they told me and they said I wasn't to get

too upset, they'd make sure I was all right and everything.
  I said: Oh yes! I'm sure!

You don't really consider your health, that your work could
ruin it, these people who do piece-work, for example, they
don't think of the consequences; you just work away so
you've got something to show for it and that's that. And the
person who thinks: No, I want to work at a normal speed, I
want to be a normal person, his health won't go downhill so
quickly, he's still in control of himself, but the others aren't.
It's the same with everything, everywhere you care to look,
it's just the same. The ones at the top help each other out, but
the ones at the bottom, they can't get anywhere, or the only
ones who can get somewhere are the more, how should I put
it, the more spiritual ones, I mean, the ones who've got a
certain amount of intelligence, who think about things. You
can't call it craftiness, that never helped anyone really, with
craftiness you always get to the point where it starts to defeat
itself. Anyway, people like us who aren't as well educated, we
often can't keep up, and that's bad.'

Oh Frau Gerster! Even someone more 'spiritual' whose
intelligence has been trained and developed comes to the
conclusion when he starts to reflect, that his own efforts are
letting him down. The more he understands the more uneasy
he becomes, all the way up your ladder, a ruthless struggle,
even right at the top.
  There must be some way of living that's fairer, more
meaningful.
  You say, politicians say it will come in time, but it won't be
easy.
  A meaningful way of living. What looks like laziness, what I
myself regard as sloth and find distasteful and for which I
reproach myself — maybe it's just the thought of all the
nonsense and overproduction which hinders my work. What's
the point of all the effort, even if people like you, Frau

Gerster, do see it as a gift, a talent which no one can take away from me? When all's said and done, it's still an effort even if it was easy, even if I was full of conviction when I started. And what's the use of it if there's already more than enough of the kind of work I might, if I'm lucky, complete one day, if there's already enough of whichever of my attempts happens to be successful.

Is this how things really are? You would say I ought to stand up for my talents. And you want to finish telling me Karl's story. So I can express the ideas for you, write about them, inform people about all sorts of things they might or might not like, so it can fulfil an inner need to communicate, as well as the one to impart knowledge.

Then there are the ones who play two roles, like Karl's father: he was always polite when he was with us but he changed the moment he left, just like Karl did later on, away at work all week and then Saturday and Sunday with me. His mother knew he was doing his duty, she told me herself: I'm so pleased he can be with you on Saturdays and Sundays, so I know where he is. But one time she came storming down to the lake in a real temper and told me she was never going to let Karl come again, I was exploiting her children and it was outrageous how little I paid them, that was the time Karl went to France. Before he went he took the foreign money from my desk, all notes. So I just said to her: Karl has some money to pay back to me and it's a private matter, between the two of us.'

Elements of this story can be swapped around like those of my own life: occurences repeated time and time again, like the roar of the engine now across at the mechanic's, the roar repeated at shorter and shorter intervals, rising to a crescendo, then the squeaking of the brakes. Old notes written down anew. Sensations repeated daily, with slight variations, which arouse the same feelings time and time again, involuntarily, feelings I can do nothing about. It doesn't matter whether I close the windows or leave them open, I will freeze or swelter but the smell doesn't only come in from outside. States of health, of illness, of well-being, the desire or the reluctance to work, feelings I ignore, don't want to acknowledge, but which prey on me nevertheless, until I feel utterly defeated, until I capitulate. Those damned engines!

Yet sometimes everything that penetrates my nose, my ears, my eyes seems to be the expression of my own being, a projection of my own personal feelings. Perhaps another person would react in quite another way to the same events, would experience them quite differently.

'You have to let a person be himself, leave him as he is. There's nothing else you can do. If he's bad you still have to treat him well and if he's a nice person, so much the better.

One man's bread is another man's . . . Anyway, Frau Gerster forgave Karl the first time he stole from her, 'because every child gets tempted some time or other and you shouldn't always rush in and make a big thing of it. And there'd never been so much as a penny missing from the boat-hire money, never, he'd never kept any back, he knew he had to enter the time on a sheet of paper, when they set off and when they came back, if it was half an hour or a whole hour. Old Charlie used to play the boss when I was away: Hey, you do this, you do that, If Frau Gerster comes back . . . ! But Karl still liked him. I sometimes said to Karl: Let him feel he is someone, just think, he's done nothing but work all his life and no one's ever really cared for him, and Karl still liked Charlie and went along with what he said. That's why I had no idea about what was going on, but his mother did. The money tallied right up to the very last week, that's why I had this trust in him and never dreamt he'd steal the most precious thing I've every been given.

And usually I always notice what's going on. I'm still quite sharp, always have been, even as a child. My father used to say to me: You'd make a good policeman.'

My father would not have said that.
   Might it not be that I imagine I know something?
   I don't bother to ask that question any more, I know I'm
constantly asking myself whether I'm imagining my knowledge,
whether I really know anything other than my doubts about
that knowledge. My father used to question almost everything I
said before accepting it.
   When I write I can read it through, check my 'knowledge'
later. What I don't understand is why my feelings are of so
little use to me, why I am seldom, if ever, able to use my
'knowledge' to guide my actions. From this I conclude that
it's not real knowledge I'm talking about. I don't know the
real truth. I think I know I could write or paint, if . . . yes,
if . . . and I have tried to verify this, have tried to test myself
by writing a book, then another book, a few poems, radio
plays, and by drawing and sculpting, and by going on
sculpting and writing. But language can resist: that's doubt.

'It's true, the kind of things I see just can't be explained. I
could be in an enormous crowd, there could be 50,000 people
there, and if there was one person there with any evil
intentions, murder or something, I'd sense it and watch him
even if he was fifty, sixty feet away, it's something or other,
perception is what it's always called. And you're born with it,
it's not something you can learn. Of course, you can develop
it, exploit it, but you shouldn't, I never would, because you
can never tell, that person might mend his ways, you musn't
risk denouncing someone, I wouldn't give anyone away,
that's their own business, it's a matter for their own
conscience. But at that moment when I'm sitting there and
someone comes and sits next to me I can always tell, it doesn't
make any difference if they're foreign or whether I speak to
him or not. It's a gift I've got, you see. Perception, that's what
it's called. That's why I can always sum a person up

immediately, I always know what kind of person he is. I can never tell where it's going to happen or when.'

At the moment I can't find any talent in me, or perception, only a growing fatigue.

Not once this whole summer, our second one here, did we go for a walk down the beautiful heathery lane towards the lake, not once did we go across to the island or out rowing on the lake or swimming. We hardly ever went out, scarcely left the house, we haven't walked down many of the lanes round here for a year now, we've missed a lot of marvellous views. Hardly speak to the neighbours now, at most a quick nod in greeting to one or other of them. Since we stopped building we've retreated into the house, into our work, hardly shown ourselves, don't even know who lives next door now the young Spaniards have left. The tenants have already changed two or three times. The lady next door is hardly ever there, I'd like to learn more from her about her friend, Madame Serova, but she's moved to her daughter's and is rarely to be seen. Sometimes when I'm getting the train to Biel she gets out of the train, coming in from Neuchâtel.

'The bit about the Du Lac, about the window, have you got that? We found out about it afterwards that time. One Sunday the weather was really bad and I said:

We're not staying here with the boats in this wind, let's go for a walk. So we went round the Du Lac along the lakeside, and when we were behind the hotel Karl asked me:

Do you know which window they broke to get in?

How could I know? You can imagine, the manager didn't wait for a carpenter to come, it was seen to immediately. Afterwards he says to me:

They were trouble-makers, real good-for-nothings they were to do that.

They didn't get away with much, thirty-seven francs is all

they got, I said. The nerve of it, asking me if I knew who'd done it! He was there with them, but that didn't come out until later, they took the keys as well, he and his friend did, all the hotel keys, and threw them into the lake, they were all special safety keys so they had to fit new locks on every door in the Du Lac and it cost the owner about three thousand five hundred francs.

The proprietor, he used to ring me up about the trips, I'd go along and see how many people had come, if you had a coachload of twenty-eight, thirty people you could reckon on some wanting the boat trip, the rest were always scared.

The repairs cost the proprietor about three thousand two hundred, maybe even five hundred and they had to pay it all back, the two of them did. The other boy, his friend, got a loan from his parents and was able to repay it all at once and now he's got to pay them back bit by bit; I expect Karl's father had to pay as he was still a minor.

We went home after the walk, I gave him something to eat as usual and he talked to me about it, about the break-in, as if it was two other people who'd done it. I didn't suspect a thing! When he was helping me with the boats he could always eat with me, he used to help me and then he'd go back into town in the evening, to his room, and then he'd come back next morning. On that last day I sent him up to the house to get a screwdriver and a pair of pliers, he was really at home with us, we had such trust in him, and that's when he took my lovely necklace. All sorts of other things as well, things I couldn't find later when I went to look for them, and it was all him. Then they both made for the town.

The place where he was doing his training, he was apprenticed to a hairdresser in Lausanne, he worked with a lady who was also a detective and because things weren't too good at home, there was never any peace at mealtimes, they were always rowing, she told him she had a room and if he couldn't stand it any longer he could go to her place, she was a divorcée. But she was on the look out for young boys, the kind who took drugs, who did all kinds of terrible things, you wouldn't believe what some of them get up to. She used to see to them, but she wasn't a social worker, she was a detective, she was even down in the phone book as one, and she let her room to him.

She had three poodles and she used to show them at dog shows and she was always winning prizes, lovely little gold spoons which were all engraved, and they were quite valuable, and after a while she couldn't find the case with the spoons in, the prizes for the lovely dogs. So even she'd had enough of Karl before long.'

A Karl as the root of all evil. I wish I was the sort of person who could always pinpoint the cause of something going wrong in other people, in something external. No, I don't really wish that. I've got toothache and I know I eat too many sweet things and don't clean my teeth afterwards. The pain gets worse because I'm afraid of the dentist. It's always my own fault and I know that whenever I try to use a scapegoat it won't be long before it comes back at me twice as hard.

'I should keep out of it, that's what the authorities told me, when they saw how ill I was. I shouldn't worry about him any more. I wrote this letter for the lawyer at the juvenile court, so at least he had something to go on, so he would know more about the circumstances. 'The story of a broken family.' And you can read it, you can use it, all you have to do is put in different words, different names, you don't necessarily have to use a different lake, merely some family X, the way I wrote it, just like I told it to you. It gives you such a marvellous feeling of satisfaction, it's like building a boat: you see it in its first stages, then you go on building until it's ready at last and you've created something which will give pleasure, something people will enjoy. And you can actually see them enjoying themselves and that's a wonderful feeling, believe me. In the old days, when I'd got the boat all smartened up like new, I used to think: O.K., you can let people on now. And when they came they always said: What a lovely boat! That means more than anything money can buy. It gives your soul, your life a real inner satisfaction. It's the same in any profession and I always say: Why do people learn a skill? It's because of that inner drive, that need to accomplish something which will give pleasure to other people, even if they don't show it, even if they keep it to themselves. That's always my reason for doing something, no matter what. And *you* can express that, *you* can get that across to people, so I've always thought: why not help you do that?'

Yes Frau Gerster, you enjoy telling me stories and you want to make a point, you want to prove something, but I'm not sure that it will give other people the same enjoyment.

I don't have that 'marvellous sense of satisfaction with my own life' that you have, that feeling is completely foreign to me, it's a feeling I very rarely get, in spite of that 'inner drive to accomplish something', to be creative.

Perhaps we should have joined forces, Frau Gerster, pretended we weren't real people, you a pleasure-boat owner and me an author. Pretended we didn't have two clearly distinguishable lifestyles and approaches to life, two separate I stories.

It's not the time for I stories, yet the success or failure of human life rests entirely with the individual and nowhere else, Frisch says.

For the sake of change we should have fused with each other, like a character in a book: Your energy, your self-confidence, your perspicacity, and added to this my small measure of critical sense (a dog is not a child and a child is not a worker and a crisis is not a natural phenomenon), my uncertainty, you and I joined as one person, that would probably have got us further, we would have gone in a different direction, a better one.

'Karl is basically a very nice child, but he's gone astray because of everything he's been through. He started going round with these people, these men, these homosexuals and there was all the stealing as well, he fell into some really bad ways. But he's got a legal guardian now, he had to go to borstal and a captain in the Salvation Army has taken responsibility for him, he thought he could convert him, set him on the right path again. As long as he's in his care he'll be all right, but I don't think he'll come back here when he's free again. He has to finish his apprenticeship, he was going to become a hairdresser, he had such a good profession all lined up and then he went and did such stupid things.

I had a little keepsake from my relatives on father's side, they were all deported during the war in France. Wherever the Germans passed through they just took everyone with them who didn't do exactly what they were told, they were simply rounded up. If someone from the village or the town said: that's one of them, he's anti-German, they just drove off with them, that's all it took. My cousin was a seamstress and one day an officer came along, he didn't bother to ask her where she got her material from, she was just ordered to make white shirts for the officers: We need so and so many shirts by tomorrow, that's all he said, so she sewed and sewed and had to use all her linen on shirts for the German officers. Her mother told her: Do what they tell you or it'll be the end of us. The men went to Vichy and they caught them there. My cousin's husband was an officer and was in the trenches, my great aunt hid with all the children during the attacks and they deported all the men, they took them to Dachau, just bundled them into lorries and took them away.'

Just like gypsies, said a refugee from the Backa region, near to tears.

The refugees were camping in front of the kindergarten in our town, you could hardly call it a square, more of a wide street, crammed with covered wagons instead of the usual market stalls. Between the wagons they had lit fires, the women were cooking on them and we stood around these strange people in their lambskin coats. Farmers from the Backa, all they had left was what they'd managed to pile hurriedly into their wagons, any food they could carry, some linen, crockery, a chicken, the grandmother, the children and a dog. Because they came from the plains their wagons had no brakes, there was snow where we lived, the mountain roads were icy and they had to use wooden cross bars which they rammed between the spokes of the wheels. New convoys kept arriving, the farmers all had the same tales to tell: the farm back home, the cows they'd left behind, the lowing cattle, the untended fields. They themselves, like gypsies in their makeshift wagons. Farmers are not gypsies.

I can't remember where the Backa is, I'll have to look it up: *Backa Hung. Bácska, Serbo-croat. Backa Yugosl. region betw. Danube and Tisza, N. Serbia. Predom. German until 1945; maize, wheat, sunflowers.*

A few months later, when the Russians from whom they had fled were stationed not far from us — although they weren't in the least 'stationary', they were advancing rapidly — the treckers, the ones we'd spoken to and many others, came back. Exhausted by their endless journeying and much poorer. They had no chickens left. And no hope.

The second picture in my old leather-bound album is of one of those covered wagons which belonged to a family I had befriended the first time they journeyed through our town — if you can call it a journey, more of a flight. The goat behind the wagon is, I think, in fact a dog, and the child running after the dog and the wagon is me. I was quite serious about it and the farmer kept trying, unsuccessfully, to turn me back. We'll never find anywhere to settle, he said. When we had passed out of the Rosental, an area I knew well, he said to me: If you run you can still be home before dark, your mother will be getting worried. Then, half-way to Landskron: Look, we'll be starving soon. You can't get anything from the fields in April. I got home only a little later than usual, hungrier than usual and no one was worried even though it was already dark, it was often quite late when I got back from the farm where I worked on the days I wasn't at school, which were becoming increasingly frequent.

I can still remember my thoughts when I was drawing that picture a few months later, by which time I had already realized that I wasn't strong enough for farm work and also that I would have to go away. I thought: If one does have to travel, if one does have to criss-cross from country to country, why wasn't I born a gypsy? But of course if that had been the case I would probably long since have perished.

'And they held out. I did everything I could to find them, I went to the Red Cross and I wrote letter after letter and in the end I was able to bring them all together again and all of them, all my cousins, clubbed together and bought me the lovely necklace as a keepsake, to thank me. And he knew about it and he stole it from me. After the trial, when they'd sentenced him, Karl that is, they rang me up, I couldn't be there because the whole business had made me ill, and they told me to go along to this shop and that shop, but he'd given false addresses and they all said they'd never seen a boy of that description, all the jewellery shops I went into. It was the only necklace of its kind, they'd paid a lot of money for it and that's what upset me. Because he knew how fond I was of it. That really galled me.

A lot of these relatives are dead now. He even made off with my husband's wedding ring.'

The fact that I'm constantly coming back to the same theme, even when I'm writing about all kinds of different incidents, *a block of dead conversations, fleeting despair*, so much so that for two years now, much longer probably, possibly right from the beginning, I could easily have identified what it is that hurts me, what it is I'm afraid of, if only I knew a name for it. As with Frau Gerster's stories, I can take the different elements of my own story apart and insert them somewhere more appropriate or more contradictory, ignoring her stories.

In almost every household here, you only have to ask, there's the story of a departure, many departures, journeys from Italy, Spain, ten, fifteen years before, and hurried, impending return journeys.

> *Travellers of the antarctic south, laden*
> *with bunches of flowers and hens,*
> *maybe they were murdered,*
> *maybe they wore out the coaches*
> *with the fire of their carnations:*
> *maybe I'm travelling and am with them,*
> *maybe the smoke of the journeys,*
> *of the wet rails, maybe*
> *everything lives on in the motionless train*
> *and I, a slumbering passenger,*
> *am unfortunately awake.*

The foreign workers can read the newspapers just as I can: *As long as underprivileged Swiss citizens — and there are many of them who have been hit by the most recent economic and social trends — direct their resentment against foreign workers who are equally underprivileged instead of declaring their solidarity with them, these foreign workers will remain the scapegoat.* They can read the newspaper reports but they can't vote on the 'reduction of the immigrant worker population', 'to protect the native Swiss', and the 'reduction of the number of permitted naturalizations'. They have no voice where their own fate is concerned.

A young Italian woman tells me how she feels, of her uncertainty about whether it would be best to leave right away with her family, two school-aged children, and go to one of the larger towns in the Abruzzi where there is still work to be had, even if it's not good work, or whether they should stay until they are forced to leave — maybe it won't even happen, maybe her husband will be able to keep his job. Being somewhere just waiting for the order to leave, that's something I know. Admiring the blossom-covered trees in the garden one last time. Sewing or planting something you might see starting to grow but are unlikely to harvest.

The voters of Switzerland yesterday rejected only too emphatically the attempts of the Republicans and the National Action to pave the way for further foreign infiltration, writes the *Baseler Zeitung,* Monday, 14th March 1977. *Is foreign infiltration a matter which must still concern us?* The article ends on that uneasy, unsettling note which is always lurking somewhere and which is always achieved at the foreign workers' expense: *For the next move towards further infiltration of foreign workers — even such a strong vote against such a move cannot obscure the fact — is definitely on its way.*

Gian can paint over the newsprint, use it for sketching paper, the news of the third vote about the fourth move towards further infiltration.

Perhaps it is because of me that I hear the same stories so often.

Maybe the lady next door only tells me about her flight from Russia because she can tell that I understand, because I know as well as she does what it's like to be driven away from your home in a Red Cross lorry. I won't tell you how hungry we were, she says. That was 1922.

And Eliette's mother, she comes from Russia too, from the Samarkand region; she tells me stories about Samarkand and how, this was before 1914, she travelled via devious routes to Switzerland and finally ended up in the Tessin. Her story, everything I heard one sunny afternoon on a terrace near Ascona, would fill a book: You should write it down, you could make a story out of it, says Eliette's mother. She paints a vivid picture of a Russian Orthodox mass in the splendid great hall of a large house, a former monastery in Moscia.

The same building where I'm spending a working week with my pupils. The class, which has now gone up into the sixth form, their form teacher and myself are sifting through all the material, all the interviews, collages and stories the pupils wrote a year ago and are now trying to put into a book. Every day some of them go out to supplement the work with fresh interviews; they question artists and eccentrics in Ascona and ladies in villas which can only be reached by private cable car. The pupils develop a skill in approaching people and in getting information out of them which any journalist or writer would envy. In the end, instead of me teaching them, I'm the one who learns from them. We are forever coming across people who just seem to have been waiting for the opportunity to say: 'You can write that down and make a story out of it.'

In little groups of two or more we sit in the garden, by the lake, in the rooms and dictate, type on four typewriters, read. The teacher, (a friend of mine whom I have to thank for this work, he delegated his class to me for six months), the pupils and I have barely enough time to get through all the new material. I read day and night, and as I do so I remember all the stories about Gero and I promise a contribution for the book. Afterwards some of the pupils even come along to help me write Frau Gerster's story.

As Eliette lives near Moscia I went to visit her. Yes, she had been taken to Moscia by her mother to attend an Easter mass. All the Russians in the area had come, some from much further afield: Christ is risen! they greeted each other instead of 'Happy Easter'. The great entrance hall had been cleared of furniture and was full of people praying fervently in front of the altar, everywhere. Eliette remembers an intricately patterned wood floor more than anything else, probably because she was very small and was hemmed in between all the adults. There was a lot of beautiful singing and there were little rolls instead of the wafer. The two nieces of the famous Verefkin came to sing, adds Eliette's mother, and the priest came from Geneva specially. No, she corrects me later, as if I really was going to put it all into a story, there was a famous priest there, but Father Joann, as a certain Prince Kurakin called himself, Otjez Joann, had come from Milan not

Geneva. Like all orthodox priests he was addressed as *batyushka*, 'little father'.

But I can't find the splendid great entrance hall. The house has since been turned into a protestant home, probably by some pious protestant designer or architect.

'The bit about the hotel in Geneva, have you got that yet?' When it's Frau Gerster telling the stories things are rather different. 'Anyway, Karl and his friend went off to Geneva and took a room in the biggest hotel, the Elite. I knew the other lad as well, he came from a Spanish family, the mother's Swiss, good people, they've got him on a tight rein now, under good control, he can't do just as he pleases any longer. Anyway, they stayed in Geneva over night, but they've got tourist police there who check the hotels. The porter had already said: Hold on a minute lads, you're too young.

But we've only come to spend the night here, to have a look, we don't know what big hotels are like. And that's where they caught them. Next morning they took the breakfast to their room; one of them was in bed and the other one was sitting at the table already, so they said, and breakfast arrived and they both got back into bed and had their breakfast there and then there was a knock at the door. The police, they'd checked the register. The elder one, Karl, gave his address and the police questioned them. The boys said they just wanted to find out what it was like in a hotel, especially Karl, he'd never been in a hotel before. But the police have to check and they asked which of them was playing the woman, they tried to make something sexual out of it, so they got cheeky with the police then and rightly too, it would never have occurred to them that they were sexual. That was the Friday night and on the Saturday Karl came to me and said they'd spent the night in the Hotel Elite and that they'd probably done a stupid thing but he wanted so much to see what it was like in a hotel. And I can understand that.

For example, we had a room for fifteen francs and I tell you, the Queen of Belgium herself couldn't have a nicer room! There was a bath and a telephone and we had a television as well, and a bell for room service and we had breakfast brought to our room in the morning, all for fifteen francs.

Wollenberg found it for us, as I told you before, he was delighted when we rang him. His sister was getting married that day though and when we rang they were just setting off for the church. He told us to wait until he got back, he was going to the church with his sister, there were about eighty guests, and he'd be able to slip away later to help us.'

The story of the church on the second floor of our house.

In what is now the children's room, painted with palm trees, castles and sailing boats, that's where they used to have their services, the lady from next door tells us. For Madame Serova hadn't used the front room, the one overlooking the street, as a bedroom any more after her husband died, she retreated to the back room, the green one, which was also warmer in winter because of the kitchen.

All the orthodox worshippers used to gather in the front room which had been cleared of furniture. I wonder what they did with the two big beds and the rest of the furniture. A Russian priest would come from Lausanne, from Bern, Geneva or Zurich, whoever was available. He heard the confessions and celebrated communions and masses. A dozen or so Russians from the area would all congregate here, my neighbour tells me. Christ is risen! A service in this shabby room disfigured by all the cracks in the walls? I find it difficult to picture religious ceremonies. They have lost all meaning for me, my year is no longer marked by church festivals, time threatens to flow away from me like a bloated body without a corset. Instead of celebrating Easter, Christ is risen!, I'll be writing.

We're sitting in our neighbour's living room, which backs on to my room. With her daughter's help she has just painted the lovely rococo woodwork green with a paler relief. Because the building was converted towards the end of the last century the stairway is lit from a skylight: Look, the sun even shines in through the inside kitchen windows for a while in the mornings, and her washing dries in the shaft of light.

But the clothes lines on the first floor are bare. The young Spaniards who lived there had given her two months' rent in advance before they went home for Christmas, it was the ideal flat for them, they told her, they really liked it, with the big terrace where the two children could play, there was even room for a paddling pool in summer. But then a telegram arrived from Spain: they couldn't get their work permits renewed, they weren't being allowed back into Switzerland.

'So we stayed in the Paradise until he could find us.' I'm with Frau Gerster again. 'He was so pleased, was Wollenberg, he said I was to stay with the luggage, I wasn't to leave, we had cases and all sorts of things with us for my daughter's trip to England, I wasn't to leave the Paradise he told me, he knew of a hotel with very good service and everything, he said he'd be right back, in about eight minutes. And my daughter went with him and they thought that the two of them wanted to sleep together, there was an old man at the reception desk and he said:

I'm sorry but we don't take such people here, this is a respectable establishment, you can have separate rooms but you can't sleep together.

And Dorli says to him: *Non, c'est pas pour ceci*, it's not for that, because I'd always told her: You must tell things as they really are. Fine. So she told him she was going to fetch her mother and would be back with her soon but that she wanted to see the room first. And that's where we stayed!'

I'm sitting in my neighbour's rococo room admiring the plants on her window ledge, ferns, a rhododendron, a rubber plant, a cyclamen. All year round you can see flowers at this window, behind the glass in winter, in front of it in summer, and when nothing's in flower there are plastic flowers, tulips.

My neighbour gets up and goes through into the kitchen, shakes the chips in the frying pan, yes, she says, she's back now, she'll always be there at weekends because that's when the children come. She's got time to chat now, they won't be here till around one.

This cupboard door, she'd always kept it open so Madame Serova could knock when she needed something. Madame Serova was often in this room, she tells me, she used to go in and out of the flat as often as she wished, she'd been really at home here.

The writing on the back of the *dacha*, the cardboard calendar, what does it mean?

They're dates, birthdays or saint's days — hers is on it, here.

And on the back of the picture of Lake Lucerne? That's a recipe. I wanted to ask her for the recipe, but instead she tells me her story about what they ate in 1922 in order not to starve. She tells me enough, too much, I don't feel like asking for the recipe any more. There had even been cannibalism, yes, it had really gone that far. You couldn't let the children go out of doors on their own, some of her classmates had been made into sausages, yes really, she had always been taken to school and brought home by her mother.

Her father had left here and gone to Russia as a private tutor, he'd fallen in love with a Russian girl there and married her. That's how they came to be transported back here as 'foreign Swiss'.

Madame Serova had fled in the other direction from a completely different region on the other side of Russia. *I went, looking for secrets, lost objects.*

On the thin gold-embossed album with the green chord which I show my neighbour there's the English word 'Photographs'. Maybe it was sent to Madame Serova from America, like the newspapers.

Those were her sons in the first picture, my neighbour tells me. The Serov sons are sitting on garden chairs in front of a wall covered with wild vines, the younger one, dark-haired with sad eyes, a tiny moustache, has his hands folded on his lap, the older one, balding, holds a little boy, a bigger one is standing next to him.

That Russian orthodox cross, a big sculpture made of ice, that's in Siberia, she tells me, yes, and the procession next to the cross which has a pigeon sitting on it, that must be in Siberia as well. Madame Serova was from one of the remotest parts of Siberia, near the Chinese border. She was a peasant, a simple woman, married to a farmer there, but she never talked about him.

The next picture shows a baptism. Look, that's how adults are baptized, in the river. You jump straight into the water which splashes up all around, and someone there is removing his white shirt. At the front of the picture, two bare chests and one head in the water, centre-back, in front of the congregation, men and women in fur hats, a priest in a white robe. The fur caps with their ear flaps suggest cold, I shiver at the sight of the half-naked people being baptized. In the photograph below is the crowd again, presumably walking home after the ceremony, little groups of white clad priests among the dark clothes, a few right at the back, at the top of the picture, still standing or wading in the shallow water, and in the foreground, upholstered objects scattered here and there, probably sedan chairs. You're more or less in China there, says my neighbour.

'Anyway, Karl went straight to Geneva that last Friday and he turned up again here on Saturday. We gave him lunch because he'd helped me all week and he wouldn't take any money. I said to him: Listen Karl, take the money! No, no. I'd never have guessed he'd stolen from me — but anyway, afterwards, that Saturday afternoon he and his friend sold the necklace and the rest and we've never been able to discover where they sold them, we suspected one jeweller but he denied it and what's gone is gone.

That Monday morning he went to the swimming pool in Lausanne and he stole something there, yes he took more things from the changing rooms. He went through some coat pockets and he took a wallet from someone, a German I think, a foreigner at any rate, and there were two thousand francs in it. That really was proper stealing that time.

It's the television that does it, that's where they get it from, these children would never think of it otherwise. Even nine, twelve year-olds, that's a really bad age for stealing and if the parents don't notice when they bring things home and don't say : Where did you get it? if parents don't get to the bottom of the problem then they've failed, they've lost the battle already. They don't develop their consciences enough at school these days, they should tell them about that kind of thing more, but if you mention it to a teacher now, all he'll say is: That's not up to us. That's a matter for the parents. But that's not true, the school and the parents must work together, after all the children are at school most of the time. And if you go shopping with little children now they even give them little baskets so they can take things themselves, and that in itself is enough to encourage them to steal, of course they'll start to think: I can take that and run off and no one will see me, it's an instinct with children, something we have to correct. If parents are only interested in having a good time and they don't bother to develop a conscience in their children, tell them what's right and what's wrong, then it's not at all surprising and things are going to get even worse. It's going to get so bad that you won't feel safe anywhere any more.'

Yes, my neighbour recognizes his face, a rather embittered face, that's the Serovs when young with their two boys. That's her second husband and he wasn't a farmer, he was a train driver in China. (According to Eliette's translation of the Russian on the back, however, it is 'a picture to show you how your children and grandchildren look now').

The married couple sitting smiling at the edge of a well, a little older.

A little boy in Chinese clothes in a toy car.

The next one, a very formal picture, a group portrait, like a commemorative monument; a small boy, another one in another little car, the mother with a scarf round her head, the father, his hands in his pockets and wearing a peaked cap, they're standing in front of a stone statue on the top of which there are two children holding a garland which reaches up to the frame of the picture.

A beaming little girl with long thin plaits, a coronet of flowers on her head and embroidered flowers all over her white dress.

The middle-aged Serova looking contented in front of a rubber plant. She could be in my aunt's living room, or at her neighbour's; the rubber plant, boring, never flowering, ever green, has become popular all over the world, no one could say where this picture was taken. The one in the picture is old with lots of off-shoots, I count at least five points, and when I think that with each new pale green leaf, its slow unfurling and opening was a real occasion and that to break off one of those points was a real crime!

An open coffin on a cart in the foreground of the next picture. The children stand around the coffin and another one leans on the arm of a young woman wearing a headscarf, two sad-looking, bare-headed Chinese are standing there and a few more women in headscarves, a few more children. I don't know who's being buried, says my neighbour.

Next to that one, a boy sitting proudly on a beautiful wooden horse.

Two sisters, you can tell, about thirty years old.

A portrait of one of them, postcard size. This is me, your loving Katya, she had written on the back of the card: At last I have made up my mind to have a photograph taken. But I look terrible in the picture and the paper's bad too. I'm forty-eight today and you can see how old I've become. I look terrible. Always your Katyenka.

She really does look bitter and angry.

So Karl had been stealing, just like a child who tried to take Frau Gerster's purse from her basket: 'Have I told you that one? I went to the post office and took my basket with me with my jacket in it and on top there was my purse where I had the paying-in slips. I was standing there chatting to someone when all of a sudden I felt something there, something strange, and it was a hand. I turned round and the child made for my purse and I said:

What do you think you're doing? And the child said it needed money, it didn't have any money. Do you know what you're doing, I said and I gave her a real slap round the face: And that's to teach you that not everyone will let you get away with it! I grabbed her arm and really let her have it: Aren't you ashamed of yourself? I get my pension, go to pay my bills at the post office and you take my money from me! And what for? Cigarettes? Drinks with the boys? Let that be a lesson to you! And then she said: Yes madame, you're right. I reckon she was about sixteen, seventeen:

Look at you, such a pretty girl and such a big girl, if you've got so little money then go out and find yourself a job or get a part-time job if you're training for something, instead of hanging around here looking out for purses to snatch! Really sharp I was and afterwards she stood there just glaring at me for quite a while.

Anyway, the foreign gentleman at the swimming pool reported it at once, he found the wallet empty, Karl had made off with the money. But I presume they'd already been watching the two of them for quite a while in Lausanne because that wasn't the first time they'd been stealing, there'd already been something in the papers, a warning that people, especially business people, should be on the alert because there were a couple of types around who were on the look out for gold, I read it in the paper. Yes gold, it was those two, they'd been at it a long time. Then they caught him, they suspected it was him, at the swimming pool, but they let him go, they wanted to see what he'd do, and he went off to this lady detective, to his room. Anyway, he confessed to her. I had a phone-call from her saying they'd caught Karl and that he was with the police. And of course everything came out then, everything took its course, so I reported it to the police. Before that I hadn't wanted to have an investigation just because of my necklace, the one my relatives bought me.'

Worked up by all the different stories and confused by what confronts me, I've lost myself.

I note down what happens to me, what takes its course, but what I note down is only a small part of what is happening around me and in me, of what is happening as a matter of course, inevitably, of what I want to avert, to repudiate, want not to let happen.

I leave Madame Serova's friend next door and look at the photos as if it were my own album, as if the brightly coloured cards, the New Year's greetings with children waving ski sticks, the colourful eggs and chickens, sprigs of forsythia and forget-me-not, were addressed to me. I get almost exactly the same cards from the girl, the woman we went out with at night, or was it just one evening, when we were little, when we were in Italy.

The family round the Christmas tree, the old lady with the headscarf, next to her the farmer, the young daughter, in front the twins in sailor suits, it could be the Czech family I used to work for.

Next to the Russian Easter greetings and the catkins, the violets and a bell there's a very old picture of three boys. I know a picture which is almost identical, one of two boys which must have been taken round about the same time: my father with his younger brother, dressed in similar clothes, the caps and the shirts with their little collars, short trousers, well below the knee on my father and on my uncle, much more elegant, knee-length, and just as my uncle's cap sits at an angle, my father's is pulled down over his forehead in keeping with his stiff bearing, so different from the more casual way his brother stands there.

I look at the little girl and at the sight of the fair plaits I feel again the compulsory hundred daily brush-strokes from my grandmother and the tugging as my long hair is tightly plaited. Later, on my thirteenth birthday, I had all this hair cut off, only to let it grow again much later, then cut again, then grow again.

Heaven help you if you have it cut! says Gian.

The child already seems as familiar to me as a close relative, the child of a brother or sister, one I'm fond of, and I could be close to but whom I only know from pictures, have only met once or twice, briefly.

In these pictures I see people I belonged to once perhaps, people who are now dead or living a totally different life on another continent. (What's the use of news from New York, the NEW RUSSIAN WORD, lovingly, regularly sent from Richmond, M.E., what can you do with the out of date news in the UNIFICATION from Australia! I sometimes get newspaper cuttings from the U.S.A. too.) All the people I've forgotten or have tried to forget, *lost souls in the trains*, the countless people I would no longer recognize were I to meet them again, *like keys without locks, fallen under the seat*.

The very thought of the numbers, the countless people you meet in the course of one lifetime, one continuous, tranquilly flowing lifetime, seems unbearable, no, I just can't imagine it, the idea of a tranquilly flowing life.

UNIFICATION is scrawled in giant letters across a wall of the station subway, written hurriedly with a dripping brush, and on the opposite wall, and on the asphalt of the roads, JURA LIBRE! Unity. We are in the south Jura, we've come to a place where most of the people are against the new canton of Jura, they voted to stay in the canton of Bern. Shouting slogans and burning flags, hatred and threats on both sides. I saw something similar a long time ago. The graffiti are quickly painted over but keep reappearing.

'And I also went along to the department that deals with guardianships, to the president, Herr Angehrn he's called, and what his father said about me to him, I've told you that already, haven't I? I had an appointment with him, the president that is, and when I arrived he stared at me and then said:

Are you Frau Gerster?

and I said: Yes.

Are you quite sure? he asked me.

What do you mean, why should I lie, at my age, of course I'm Frau Gerster!

So you're quite sure you're Frau Gerster?

It was just like that time in Brussels with the old gentleman who kept on and on staring at me and came and sat next to me and stared, and I went over to my daughter and I gestured to her, like this, touching my head, and he just kept on staring. So I went to the toilet and Dorli stayed there and he went up to Dorli and said to her: Am I dreaming, Miss, or is it true, the lady who was just sitting there, is she alive or is she dead? So she said: That's my mother, of course she's alive! When I came back into the visitors' lounge where we were sitting, it was our second evening in Brussels, there was a television there and everything you could want, he put his arm on the arm of my chair, like this, you see, and then he kept stroking me like this. I couldn't help laughing and I said:

Ça vous fait du bien? I said to him: are you enjoying yourself, I had no idea, you see. And then, all of a sudden he said to me:

My wife was buried three days ago and you look just like my wife! Everything, just everything about you is the same, that's why I can't understand whether you're alive or dead. And I felt so sorry for the man that I took him in my arms like this and I held him to me and told him I was alive and that he could feel I was alive, couldn't he. He was the hotelier's father. And him too, just imagine, when we walked into the hotel he, the hotelier, didn't know if I was alive or dead either. And he asked if he could eat with us. And they served us at

table every day, everyone else had to serve themselves, but
they gave us a special table and served us our meals. So I said
to Dorli: Let's make sure we eat with the hotelier's father
every evening, not lunchtime though, we were always out
then. It really helped to keep him entertained, the old man,
yes, he enjoyed it and it was an experience for me. Then I
went to the plane with Dorli, she was really happy when she
left, not at all scared, and she said to me: Mummy, now you've
shown me how you find your way around in strange places. I
stayed on a few more days and he went out with me
sometimes, sometimes he felt like it, sometimes he didn't, and
he explained everything to me. He said he'd come to
Switzerland, he'd stay at the Du Lac but he didn't come, he
probably died. I think he was very grief-stricken for a long
time after I went away. He was always around us, always.
What could I do, I couldn't ignore him could I, after all, I've
been through it myself, I know what it's like to lose someone
so what was I to tell him? I told him he wasn't to get any ideas,
it wasn't long since I'd lost my husband so I wasn't thinking of
marriage or of getting involved with anyone. I said he was free
to come if he wanted but he wasn't to start thinking of
anything else.

Anyway, where were we? Yes, the president, Herr Angehrn:
You are Frau Gerster? And he keeps on and on staring at me:
So you really are Frau Gerster?

I must know why you've asked me the same question three
times. I can show you my railway pass, there's a photo on it, I
can show you my identity card, are they proof enough?

Then it's not true, what people told me, he said.

So what was it they told you?

Then he said Karl's father had said I was the kind of person
who ... well, I took in young boys between sixteen and
eighteen, I went out with them, I was the kind of woman who
wore make-up and dyed her hair, trendy clothes, and then he
said:

But it's not true, you're a granny! And I said:

I certainly am, I've got two grandchildren! Maybe you

mean the boys I had from Goldau? The first one's getting married next Saturday, I'm supposed to be going but I can't manage it. He was so mollycoddled you see, so spoilt, the first time he came to me he was a little thing and he was almost a head taller by the time he left. The way he downed his food! He's a different child now, his father told me, and all in the two months you've had him. I gave him his food, he helped me out a great deal and I paid him one hundred francs for the two months. The following year they contacted me in the spring and asked if he could come again. Yes of course Bruno could come, I'd be only too pleased. And I had the second son as well, for two or three years, it worked out fine with him as well, and later on I had the girl, they sent all the children in the family to me when they got to the last two or three years at school.

Anyway he said to me, Herr Angehrn that is: This doesn't fit in at all with what I've heard about you.

Yes well, that's not surprising if you take any notice of what they tell you, it's all lies with them. That's the first time it occurred to me, I'd never thought about it before, I had such trust in him. He was always fine with us, he took us in good and proper, our house was a home from home for him, even that last Sunday I said: Now listen Karl, if anything goes wrong, you can never tell what might happen, you know you've got a home here, you've been with us five years now and we're really pleased to have someone to do things for us, to help us out, you could ask him to do anything, absolutely anything and he'd never say no. That's why I was so terribly disappointed in him. Anyway, that's the way things are, there's nothing to be done about it. Things go wrong. You can't take everything to heart. But you do have to speak your mind.'

The man from the house insurance company is inspecting our house. He goes from one room to the next making calculations, noting down details, sizing the place up, as they say. I begged my daughters to clear up, to help me clean the place, it really did need doing badly. But you can plead, they won't do it. 'It's the way their parents bring them up.' I'd be so pleased if I had someone who would do things for me, I'd be so pleased if the flat was clean and tidy, if someone would give me a hand, but I can't ask other people, not even my own children to do things I don't like doing myself. I hurriedly gather up all the dirty clothes lying about the place, and on the stairs I come face to face with the surveyor, the bundle of dirty washing under my arm. He glances behind the wooden partition where everything except for the washing machine and the boiler is just as it was originally, and I glance at the plaster ceiling which has caved in, the dust and debris on the floor and on the washing machine: *c'est un cauchemar*, I sigh: a nightmare, and the surveyor nods. I make a quick getaway, retreat to my room, where the piles of paper on the table, on the chair, on the couch, on the cupboards and the stove have already been surveyed, but where at least I am spared the sight of this orderly gentleman actually noting down the chaos and the dust up there.

While I am staring angrily out of the window having been disturbed in my work, a yellow Mercedes pulls up across the street in front of the bank. The driver looks at a piece of paper as if checking an address, takes the steering wheel again, turns into the square and parks the car with its foreign oval number plates under the plane trees. He gets out, Chinese I think, and helps the other people out of the car, his family probably; one after the other, a slight young woman, a small boy, a bigger boy and a girl of about eleven with long, smooth black hair, all emerge. The man points to our building, perhaps to my window, and the Chinese people walk towards the house, towards me, with tired, unsteady steps, they seem to have been travelling a long way, they go round the fountain and towards the passageway.

Like the midget family which sat down next to me in an empty railway carriage a few years ago when I was writing about midgets. You know nothing about midgets, I had written an hour before, and there I was suddenly surrounded by them. There were eight of them, they were talking and gesticulating to each other, to me as well, yet I felt an outsider, I was the only person in the compartment whose feet touched the ground when sitting down. It's impossible to imagine what it's like to be a midget.

As I hurry to note this down, I'm really eager to get on with another picture from the album, I wait for the door-bell to ring.

The picture is of a woman standing next to the smiling young girl with the plaits which are so long that they hang down below the picture, a foreign-looking woman.

Chinese, says my neighbour, it's Madame Serova's sister-in-law with her niece. The girl of about eleven doesn't look Chinese nor Mongolian, and yet there's a similarity between the two faces: the same wide, remarkably high forehead, the same hairline. The fine hair is drawn back from a centre parting. The mother's plaits are black and wound round her head like a coronet, the girl's hair seems fair and is divided into two plaits on a level with her wide, smiling mouth, stiff and thin they stand away from her white collar and knotted neckscarf which I presume is red, the colour of the *Sokoln*. The 'Red Falcon' I remember and have seen occasionally on television, marching.

The mother is wearing a knitted dress, a cleverly knitted peacock design, the collarless neckline gathered towards the centre, I imagine it to be old rose. Over this a spotted pinafore with wide shoulders, the edges pinked. I found a similar pinafore among Madame Serova's clothes and kept it for myself.

The peculiar similarity between two such different faces. The smile of the fair-haired little girl has become an expression of kindness and strength in the Mongolian woman. A few wrinkles on her forehead, between her nose and mouth which don't mar the lovely face.

The door-bell hasn't rung. The yellow Mercedes is no longer down on the square, I didn't see the Chinese drive off. The woman in the picture probably isn't Chinese at all.

She could be from Lake Baikal, from Irkutsk, or she could come from Tashkent, maybe Andizhan. *Many lonelinesses had assembled there and were waiting to depart, like poor people on the platforms.* It's a long way, the journey from Tashkent or Lake Baikal to Hong Kong. The kind of journey you surely only make with a family, with small children, if you're forced to, expelled, thrown out, if you're fleeing. A journey to a country whose customs and language you know nothing about.

Even before she left China Madame Serova had become ill from all the worries and troubles, says Frau Gerster. 'They took her into hospital; she'd already had a minor stroke, the beginnings of a stroke. But as long as she was in hospital in China she couldn't make the journey, so they told her to come on to them later. She'd recovered after about six weeks and was terrified she might not be able to find her belongings, she'd hidden them in a wood. She'd probably changed all her money into gold when she left, she'd had it all made into teeth and crowns and put in her mouth. But she still had some money, a few possessions, and that's what she'd hidden and was afraid she wouldn't be able to find. But she did find it all and she took it with her sewn into her clothes because she was really scared of the customs, in case they took it away from her. But it never occurred to them that she had any money.

That's how Madame Serova managed to get straight from China to Switzerland, unlike all the others who were shunted from place to place, she was certainly here in this town for a good ten years and three or four other places before that, and in a home for refugees. They had to pay for that themselves. They had enough money, Madame Serova certainly paid her way.'

She'd certainly spent very little on herself, her friend hadn't, says my neighbour. For she sent as much as she could to Russia. Yes, Madame Serova used to send parcels to her family, all the ones who'd stayed behind in Russia, and they got there, she had proof of that. She herself lived very modestly.

'And this is what I get, nothing but ingratitude from the whole family.'

I'm at Frau Gerster's and she's going on about Karl again:

'It's all because of the way their parents bring them up. The children were afraid of both of them, of all the violence, neither of them had an ounce of sense, the way they used to hit them, neither of them was very bright and the mother was cold and hard, heartless. Now they deny everything, they're telling a pack of lies; it was Karl's fault that his mother was so ill — that was shoved under the child's nose at every opportunity. But I couldn't say anything to her. I went to see her in hospital and when I saw the terrible state she was in it was no good. It doesn't surprise me at all the way her son Karl has been destroyed. You can't talk to the father either, he's the kind who's always got a ready answer and he's completely irresponsible. So it's no wonder the children have gone wild. Since he started his apprenticeship he's got new ideas about all sorts of things, moral things and spiritual things, he's just gone to pieces.'

I don't know Karl and I only know Frau Gerster's version of the story; I don't know whether he sees himself as having gone to pieces, or what he would say about himself. And the other characters in Frau Gerster's stories, they only look like that in Frau Gerster's eyes and her imagination only exists in the way I've written her fantasies down.

But I do know, after everything I've heard from her about other people and from what I've heard from others, my neighbour or Mademoiselle Alice for instance, something about the destruction of my own brain. About the destruction of the natural ability to think clearly, coherently, the ability to form the fleeting, rushing thoughts into words and sentences and to articulate them if necessary. Destroyed by life's countless little battles, which Karl surely knows all about, destroyed by all the time lost every day, by running the home, by the daily routine, work, bad conscience, the endless conversations, laden with resignation, which demand too much defence and resistance from me. I don't want to become resigned.

They put so much pressure on the boy. That child was searching for love, tenderness, some peace. My sister and I gave him a lot of encouragement, we gave him little talks on morals but he didn't have a clear conscience and now he knows he's lost something, a great deal in us. He's only too well aware of it.

But he went to the lady detective, the one who was there for the boys and he told her he'd done something stupid, there was the money, the police would probably come and they could have the money back then. Listen Karl, she said: it doesn't work like that, you'll have to go along to the police yourself, I don't want anything to do with it. He confessed, he confessed to her and then he gave himself up, I'm not sure whether he went along there himself or whether he rang them. The police said they'd be there to pick him up on the Tuesday morning but the lady detective wasn't at all pleased about that: Oh no, not in my place, I'm not having the police in my house, I'll send him along to the railway station. And that's where they picked him up, the police, but they weren't in uniform.

I went through an awful kind of upheaval afterwards, it was because of Karl and the accident on the railway. There must be some kind of force that guides your actions, I've never really thought about it before but otherwise why did I happen to be there just at that moment, there must be, how should I put it, there must be something. Because it always seems to be the same people who have experiences like that again and again, I don't know if it's fate or not. I just notice things.

It was March but we had the boats out already, it was the end of March, no, not evening, it was afternoon, about four o'clock, the dog picked up the scent, it was an old man, he'd been on the platform and was caught by the train and fell under it and bits of him were spattered all along the rails from the station to the bridge. The dog had already got scent of it. The station was closed, the man up in the train had seen him but it was too late. Possibly he wasn't very well, perhaps he had a dizzy turn or something which made him sit down there for a moment, and it's no distance to the tracks. We can't really tell what happened, he was so mangled up. They had to hunt around to tell where he came from, he was a priest but not from these parts. He went down the station underpass and probably wanted to get across to the old people's home from the other platform. I didn't actually see it but I did say to myself: When an express train brakes like that something must have happened! It wasn't until the train had gone right through the station that the driver saw there was a person all squashed on the tracks. And the person who had to clear up put it all in a sack, all the bits of flesh, it all went into a sack.'

And so the motionless train ran
over my bones
in the painfully dawning morn.

Two years, and as I write it becomes three. The 29th March 1974, Gian scratched into the wet plaster in the studio. And underneath: Susanna. It was her fifteenth birthday. Susanna was born on Easter Sunday. Easter bunnies are in the shop windows again and I'm seized by panic at the sight of all the nests with their brightly coloured sugar eggs and chocolate rabbits; but after all, I tell myself, it's only March 1977 and I've got almost a month until Easter, the date I've set myself, until my time is up. I see and hear and note down Frau Gerster's words, which I hoped would help me, but they are having a destructive effect, are driving out the last vestiges of order.

'Each to his own,' I hear her saying.

The last pages of Madame Serova's album are set out in a peculiar, disquieting way: two pictures of the same person side by side, one really young with full, dark-painted lips, wavy hair tucked behind the ears and tumbling over the collar of her Russian smock, and one middle-aged, very serious, the hair a little shorter, mouth narrow, drawn outwards and turned down slightly at the corners, it's probably her. And on the next page, almost the same: a young boy in a long, stiff school coat, hands in pockets in front of a photographer's painted background, a seascape; to the left, next to his shoulder, climbing plants are growing in a vase on a pedestal and are twisting their way across the sea. Next to this is Monsieur Serov's picture, about fifty years later, with the same serious, slightly suspicious expression. Both of these pictures are upside down and the pictures which follow them are out of sequence, have been stuck haphazardly into the album, side by side, at all different angles or facing each other.

Is that you? the museum curator asks me and points to Madame Serova's photograph in Gian's studio.

And one man, after a reading from one of my early books, asks me about the meaning behind my writings. The various elements are all there, he says, but where is it all leading?

Why don't you just paint pictures instead of writing?

'I sometimes see pictures, I see them in front of me.' I see meanings before I've thought about them properly. 'Times when you see that it really is true, when you can experience for yourself,' when you learn and realize that it's not always only other people who get ruined, hurt, destroyed.

All the empty days when I can't work, depressed and paralysed by what I see and hear.

'That was something which really upset me. All that worry and anxiety, you can just imagine, Gero and the boy and then the accident on the railway, it all came at once. Out of the blue. We'd never noticed, never imagined there was anything wrong with him. Towards the end carrot was just about all he was eating, because he knew it was good for him. He used to eat anything, apples, pears, cherries, strawberries, sauerkraut, you have to train them from when they're little, we never gave him many sweet things.'

I can't find Madame Serova's recipe now. It must be a cake recipe, said the lady next door: a pound of flour, four cups of sugar, how many eggs? Strange that she's written flour down twice, it's very difficult to read her writing, she says, it's all scribbled. Impossible to decipher it all.

'He used to eat anything I put in his mouth. He liked raw carrots best, he ate three pounds of raw carrots every week. He could understand now why he lived so long, the vet told me, the carrots had kept him well nourished and gave him a lovely shiny coat. And he was so lively, even just before the operation he fetched his ball for a game, he summoned up all his strength at the last moment. The vet is one of the best in Switzerland, to start with he said: He's got a ruptured appendix, I'll operate. And when he cut him open he didn't bother to sew him up again, he gave him the injection then and there. He had growths in his stomach and the exit from the stomach, and on his liver and in his, what's it called, in his gall bladder, and his intestines, all full of growths. And he said to me: How did the animal last that long? He couldn't understand it. I had him thirteen years. And the worse I got the more ill he became and then I went into hospital for my operation.'

I know by heart now which tune follows which on the tape they play next door; I know their titles from my children who listen to the same ones. My neighbour says her neighbour on the other side has made recesses in the walls and her friend, Madame Serova suffered a great deal because of the music when she was ill. After 'Mr. Tambourine man' there's 'Momma, Momma' and 'Here comes the sun', 'She came in through the bathroom window'. Each lunchtime, 'Oh, Mr. Tambourine man' and every day after half past five there's 'Here comes the sun' and 'You never give me your money',

'How would you feel' — poor Madame Serova! I hum along with them when I'm in good spirits, and when I can't stand Jimi Hendrix and his 'How would you feel' coming through the wall for the umpteenth time I drown the neighbours out with my radio, with the first thing I come across, which isn't usually what I want. I haven't been really ill here yet even if I have often been desperate for some peace and quiet. Poor Madame Serova: Steppenwolf and Melanie, the Beatles and the Brotherhood of Man, all can be heard quite loudly but unintelligibly through the wall. What could the old lady do? She can't even complain. No one speaks Russian.

She knocks, she calls.

After her last stroke she knocks on the floor as best she can, but Mademoiselle Alice is hard of hearing. The Spanish baby is crying upstairs, footsteps sound as if they're passing directly above her ear. Next door Frank Zappa is screaming: 'Would you like a snack?'

She crawls as best she can, half-paralysed to the wall and knocks, 'Momma, Momma', keeps on and on knocking, her friend is away, she knocks for a day and a night until Madame Jarjema comes to visit her.

With so many incomprehensible beings
weighed down by so many deaths
I felt myself lost on a journey
on which nothing moved,
only my tired heart.

'It happened all of a sudden,' says Frau Gerster: 'the worry about the boy, the dog and that accident, it all built up, that's why the stones appeared so suddenly, in less than thirty hours. If a stone builds up gradually it's always round, but if it forms suddenly it's jagged and that sort is really dangerous. They loosened four of the stones and had to remove one. And my other operations as well: they cleaned the sclerosis out of my hip, it hadn't gone too far yet, and afterwards they did my coccyx, there was something similar there as well, I broke it years ago and there was a build-up of calcium, they took all that away neatly and put it neatly back in place. That's what they told me at the hospital just after they'd examined me, that stones can appear quite suddenly. That was because of Karl: You must have been worrying about something, they said to me, and a psychiatrist came to see me after the operation, and a priest, and they kept saying there must be something wrong and I had to come out with it. But nothing they tried was any use, I just didn't want to talk about it, I wanted to keep it to myself. I couldn't understand it, I couldn't understand how he could have done it to me because I'd had him for five years.

But he's a victim of his family. You can't know why the mother's like she is, the father will get his punishment though, there's always someone around who's more powerful than we are, who gives the orders, just be patient, let things take their own course. The father said terrible things about Karl whenever he could. And about me as well. But I'm not going to let a good-for-nothing like that make me ill, he's too stupid for me; the pitcher that goes too often to the well gets broken; he who laughs last laughs loudest; reward comes to him who waits.

Early this morning, though it wasn't really all that early, the telephone woke me. It was Eliette saying she was in Basel, that she had a meeting with someone there today and that she'd like to come over tomorrow, Sunday. Yes, I say, fine, and I look for a good train: You leave Basel at 10.08 and get to Biel at 11.13, from there you take the local Neuchâtel train at 11.22 and I'll pick you up at the station.

I'd have liked a moment to catch my breath, but the characters in my novels are real people and, like myself, impatient, unpredictable. They're not easy to deal with.
How many years is it since Eliette last paid me a visit?
I can still see her walking away.